WARN

THIS BOOK IS

BOOBY - TRAPPED WITH VORPENT VENOM

DO NOT TURN THE PAGE

First published in Great Britain in hardback in 2014
by Hodder and Stoughton

This paperback edition published in 2016
by Hodder and Stoughton

Text and illustrations copyright © 2014 Cressida Cowell

The right of Cressida Cowell to be identified as the Author and
Illustrator of this Work has been asserted by her in accordance
with the Copyright, Designs and Patents Act 1988.

1 3 5 7 9 10 8 6 4 2

A CIP catalogue record for this book is
available from the British Library.

ISBN 978 1 444 92321 6

Printed and bound in China

Designed by Jennifer Stephenson

The paper and board used in this book are made from wood from responsible sources

Hodder Children's Books
An imprint of Hachette Children's Group
Part of Hodder and Stoughton
Carmelite House, 50 Victoria Embankment, London, EC4Y 0DZ

An Hachette UK Company
www.hachette.co.uk

THANK YOU to Jennifer Stephenson
and Naomi Greenwood for all
your help in the making of this book.

In The Complete Book of Dragons

(a guide to dragon species)

written and illustrated by

CRESSIDA COWELL

~ CONTENTS ~

Long ago, the world was full of dragons. Imagine them wheeling in the skies, hopping through the grasses, lighting up the caves, swimming slow and silent through the seas.

What happened to the dragons? Where are they now? These pages are taken from the notebooks of a young Viking boy called Hiccup Horrendous Haddock the Third, writing between the ages of ten and fifteen.

Hiccup's later memoirs, written when he was an old man, tell the story of the Great Dragon Rebellion, and what happened to the dragons in the end. But these notebooks paint a picture of the brilliance and fire and spirit of that lost dragon world.

Look around you at our own world now. You may not see dragons, but notice the numberless quantities of species

that we have in our woods, in the air, in the mountains, in the skies. The proud lion, the mighty elephant, the seals, the birds, the thousands of types of beetle. One of those beetles could be the cure for some terrible disease…

Take care, dear reader, that we are looking after the boundless wonder of our world.

Remember the dragons.

Cressida Cowell

MAP OF THE
BARBARIC
ARCHIPELAGO

THE ISLE OF BERK

Hooligan ship

Caliban Caves
(Do NOT go here unless you have to)

Unlandable Cove

DEATH'S HEAD HEADLAND

Wild Dragon Cliff

Hooligan Village

Madman's Gully

THE HIGHEST POINT
(recently destroyed by FIRE)

Hooligan Harbour

The Long Beach

Black Heart Bay

The Little Isles

Cowrie Beach

Hysterical ship

Puffin Point

Isles of DOOM

Wanderer ship

Bashem-Oik ship

Bog-Burglar ship

Outcast ship

Visithug ship

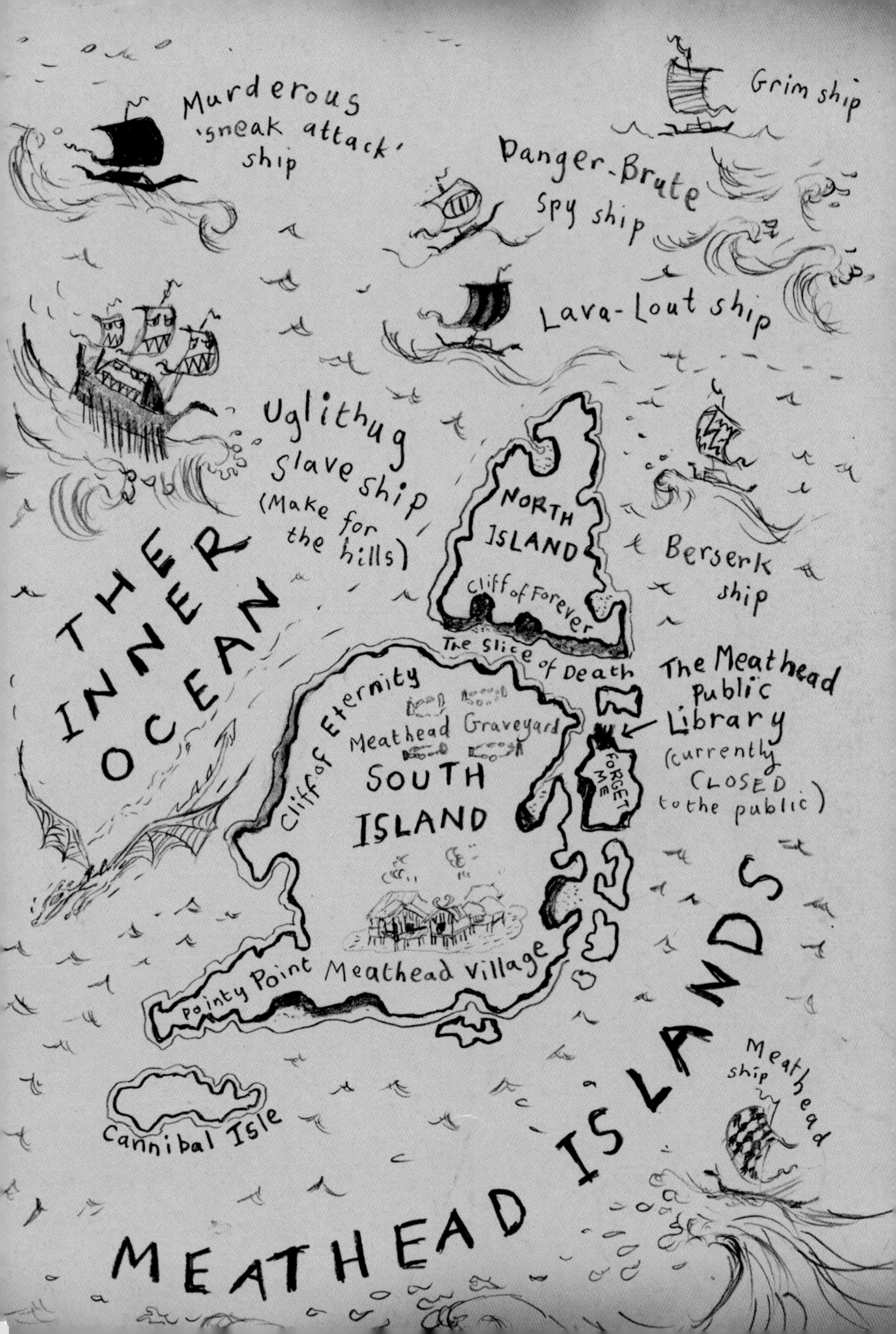

Murderous 'sneak attack' ship
Grim ship
Danger-Brute Spy ship
Lava-Lout ship
Uglithug slave ship (Make for the hills)
NORTH ISLAND
Cliff of Forever
Berserk ship
THE INNER OCEAN
The Slice of Death
The Meathead public Library (currently CLOSED to the public)
Cliff of Eternity
Meathead Graveyard
SOUTH ISLAND
FORGET ME
Pointy Point
Meathead Village
Cannibal Isle
Meathead ship
MEATHEAD ISLANDS

This is ME,
Hiccup
Horrendous
Haddock
the
Third,
and
my
hunting
dragon,
Toothless.

O.K., I have to admit, this book
isn't REALLY booby-trapped with
Vorpent Venom.
      I just said that because
this book is supposed to be a
SECRET...

I want to write books about dragons.

… but my father is always finding my notebooks and destroying them. You see, my father, STOICK THE VAST, Chief of the Hairy Hooligan Tribe, doesn't think I should be writing books about dragon species. He thinks I should concentrate on my

YELLING

What my father says is:

'Barbarians don't write books! A true Barbarian YELLS at the dragons that are his slaves, and IGNORES the rest of them. And as for speaking their horrible snaky language, Dragonese, that is strictly against the Law. What is the point of knowing the difference between an Arsenic Addywhatsit, and a Glow-bug or whatever you call them? Concentrate on your yelling, and give up this foolishness.'

But what happens if you bump into the kind of dragon on the other side of this page? (Be careful as you turn over...)

Trust me, if you try ignoring this particular dragon, it will **EAT** you...

"Yelling won't work either.

What you need in this situation is a lot of information about Hellsteethers, and you need to start speaking Dragonese FAST. That's why it is so important to know your dragons around here.

So this is why I am writing this book, describing all the dragons I know, their habitats, their anatomy, their eggs, their methods of attack and their defences. This book will tell you how to find dragons, how to track them, how to look after their eggs and their babies if they hatch. It will include all the dragon species I know, and give you tips on how to ride and train them, or to deal with them if they attack.

rucksack for Dragonwatching equipment

Book of notes about dragons

shiny mirror for dealing with Breathquenchers

I am showing you here some useful pieces of Dragonwatching equipment if you want to do a spot of Dragonwatching yourself.

Dragons are wonderful, mysterious creatures.

They are also, as you will see, ABSOLUTELY TERRIFYING.

So intelligent people should be scared of dragons, but we should also strive to understand them, because we can only defend ourselves from dragons, and live with them peacefully, if we understand them.

So let's begin by understanding Dragon Anatomy…

Telescope thingy for watching dragons from a long, long, way away

Something yellow

Glass for inspecting dragon poos

Dragonskin firesuit for fiery situations

I am a secret Dragonwatcher.

Dragons are the only creatures on earth who can exist in all 4 elements... in EARTH in AIR in SEA and in FIRE

DRAGON ANATOMY

ALL dragons are extremely dangerous – even the ones that look cute, like Toothless – and here is why.

Dragons have fireholes that can fire flames, poison darts, rocks, spears, lightning, laser beams and electric bolts. Some species are a hundred times more poisonous than a black widow spider, others give electric shocks, or have multiple sets of teeth that can actually shoot out and bite you. Some have blood made out of sulphuric acid that they can propel in jets out of their eyes.

Dragons can be so well camouflaged they are virtually invisible. They can track you down through all four elements – earth, air, sea and fire. They can smell your blood from a mile away and hear your heart beating across a mountainside.

Of course, not ALL dragons look like the dragon on the following page. Some are very teeny-weeny primitive creatures...

DRAGON ANATOMY

Dragons have 3 sets of eyelids

What You Can't See...
Some dragons are also armed with radar, and Seadragonus Giganticus Maximus can look into the future and communicate telepathically

Smoke can be two different colours

Many dragons have more than one tongue. The saliva can be poisonous.

All dragons
have gills as well
as lungs so they
can breathe under
the water. When
the gills are
working, the
lungs shut down
automatically.

The Fireholes are located at
the base of a dragon's throat. In
smaller dragons, these are invisible to
the naked eye. In some dragons, one
hole shoots fire, the other explosive gas.

Gormatroh

Giant Deathwatch

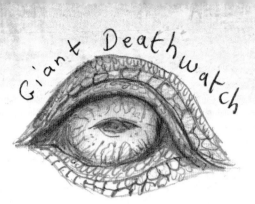

Grimler

Riproarer

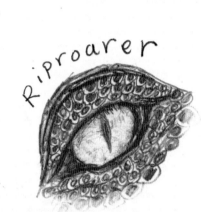

Common-Or-Garden

Deadly Shadow

Windwalker

Bullrougher

DRAGON EYES

Most dragons are equipped with what you might call
'Super-senses'. Take dragon eyes, for example. Some
dragons have multiple eyes. Others have eyes on stalks,
or eyes that can project out suddenly on the ends of long
spaghetti-like structures, so the dragon can see around
the corner.

Dragons' eyes often have a sort of x-ray vision, so that
they can see through objects like trees, and in night-time
their eyes automatically switch to a 'heat sensor' mode,
so they can track prey through their body heat.

Seadragonus
Giganticus Maximus

DRAGON TONGUES

Forked tongues are good for lying. Dragon tongues are amazingly flexible. Many dragons have more than one tongue — the Woden's Nightmare has up to thirty — each one able to distinguish a different taste.

Dragon saliva is often poisonous

Some dragons, such as
TONGUE-TWISTERS,
grow their tongues to such a
length that they can twist off
a man's arm.

Some of the sounds in
Dragonese can only be made if
you have a dragon's flexible
tongue.

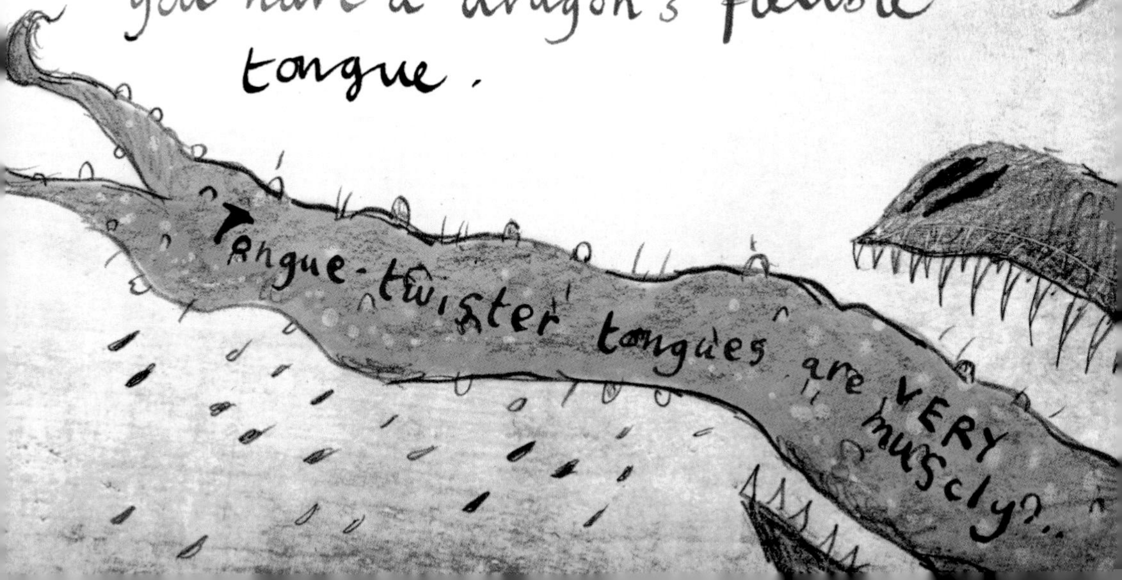

Tongue-twister tongues are VERY
muscly?...

DRAGON FIREHOLES
are not just for firing flames

Dragon fireholes are an extra-ordinary natural feature, and they are unique to dragons.

In smaller dragons they are invisible to the naked eye. These holes can also shoot lightning bolts, or spears of bone, in the case of this

MASSIVE
Leviath organ...

Deadly Shadow
Shooting lightning

Poison Sh D

In some dragons, the s shoot
poisonous or -e-x-p-l-o-..-v-é gas.

Gorebluffers swallow large stones
that are then ejected through
the fire-holes with the
force of CANNON
BALLS

This is Toothless, in a hibernation sleep.

HIBERNATION

Many dragon species, as you can see, are entirely un-trainable. But for thousands of years, Vikings have used dragons to hunt fish for us, to carry us into battle, or to pull our sleds in winter. So despite the fact that dragons are exceptionally dangerous, one of the first Initiation Tests for a young Warrior is to CATCH YOUR DRAGON.

Catching an adult dragon is an extremely bad idea. Luckily, most baby Bog, Tree, Air and Sea Dragons hibernate in gigantic caves known as Dragon Nurseries. As part of an Initiation Test into the Hooligan Tribe, we have to creep into those caves, and steal an infant dragon to train as our hunting-dragon or riding-dragon.

Dragons who hibernate are known as "Wintersleepers", while dragons who do not are "Evergreens".

The cave systems of the Barbaric Archipelago are as full of life as a coral reef, brilliantly lit by the dragons themselves and humming with noise: the busy vibration of Slugbulbs dozily drifting through the caverns, the hiss, pop and crackle of Flamehuffers blasting jets of flame to incinerate un-wary Caterbillars, and the rumbling snoring hum of the thousands of dragons who come here to hibernate.

It is important to avoid the true monsters of the underground world: the shape-changing Riproarers, and the great transparent giant, the Monstrous Strangulator, who injects venom thirty times as toxic as a black widow spider.

DO NOT WAKE UP
the infant dragons,
while you are
stealing them...

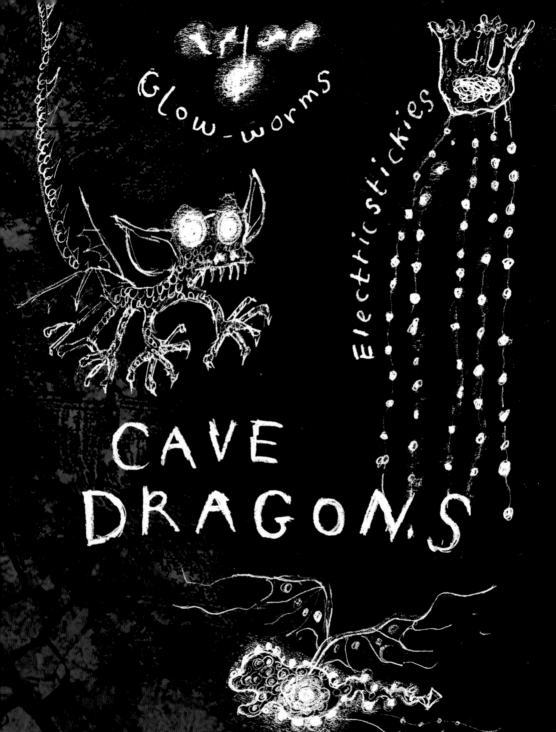

Glow-worms

Electricstickies

CAVE
DRAGONS

Slugbulbs

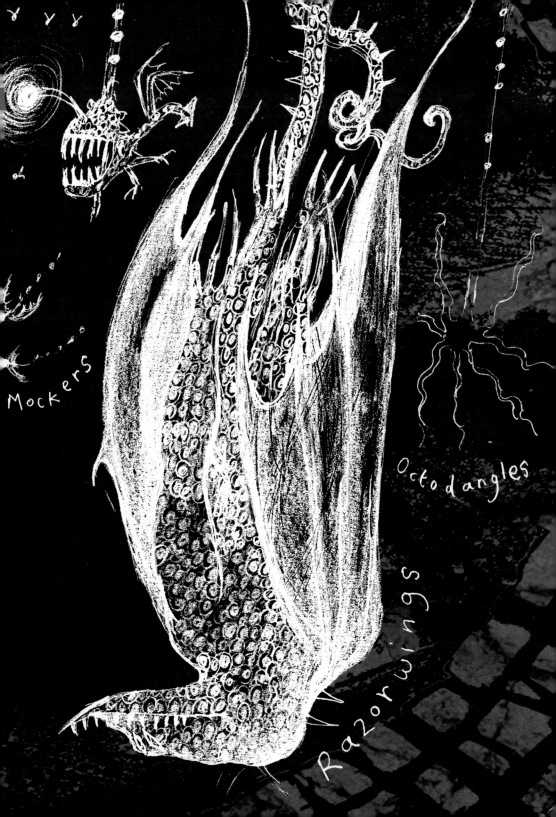

Mockers

Octodangles

Razorwings

Eight-Legged Nadders

Fear Factor: 4 Size: 3
Attack: 5 Disobedience: 4
Speed: 7

It can take days for
Nadders to untangle
themselves.

Glow-worms

Fear Factor: 0   **Size:** 0

Attack: 0   **Disobedience:** 2

Speed: 0   (they're VERY stupid)

The Glow-worm is a tiny creature that looks more like a worm than a dragon, but is still, genetically speaking, part of the dragon family. Although technically they can't be trained exactly, they are a useful source of light on moonless nights, or in caves. The Vikings use them in lanterns, to light up homes and ships in the night-time.

Glow-worms look VERY like Arsenic Adderwings... do not mistake them!

GLOW-WORM EGGS GLOWING in the dark.

Glow-worm eggs are easy to find, owing to their tendency to glow in the dark. But eating them does have unfortunate side-effects, as Toothless finds out in 'How to Train Your Viking'.

Red-Hot Itchyworms

Fear Factor: 4   Size: 0

Attack: 4   Disobedience: 3

Speed: 5

Red-Hot Itchyworms are tiny maggot-like dragons that bite considerably harder than ants or wasps. They are blood-suckers, and when they get into a person's clothing they swarm all over the body in a pack, biting incessantly. An attack by Red-Hot Itchyworms is infinitely worse than having ants in your pants. Although these dragons aren't trainable, they are often used by Vikings to protect precious objects by 'alarming' the floor with them.

Camicazi always carries a box of these Itchyworms in her Burglary Kit, because they're handy for putting down the knickers of a prison guard.

Flamehuffers

Fear Factor : 3   Size : 3
Attack :   3
Speed :   4   Disobedience : 7

Flamehuffers are mischievous little creatures
who like to cause trouble by mimicking human
voices, as well as the sounds of other animals.

Fear Factor : 7   Size : 7
Attack : 8   Disobedience : 5
Speed : 8

The Gronckle is the plug-ugly of the dragon world.
But what it lacks in looks, it makes up for on the
battlefield with its razor-sharp fangs.

THE GRONCKLE

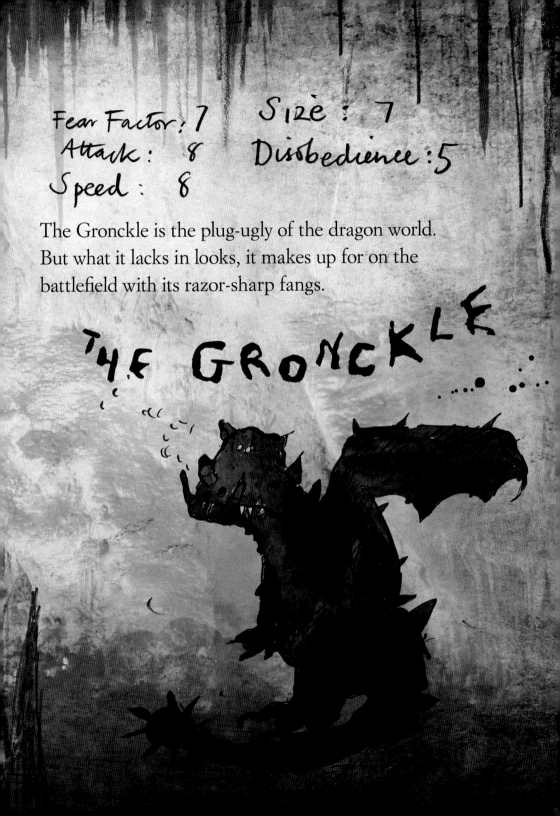

Riproarers cannot stand
the taste of parsnips
so they won't go
near you if you
have recently
eaten this
vegetable.

(Only problem is,
I can't stand parsnips either.)

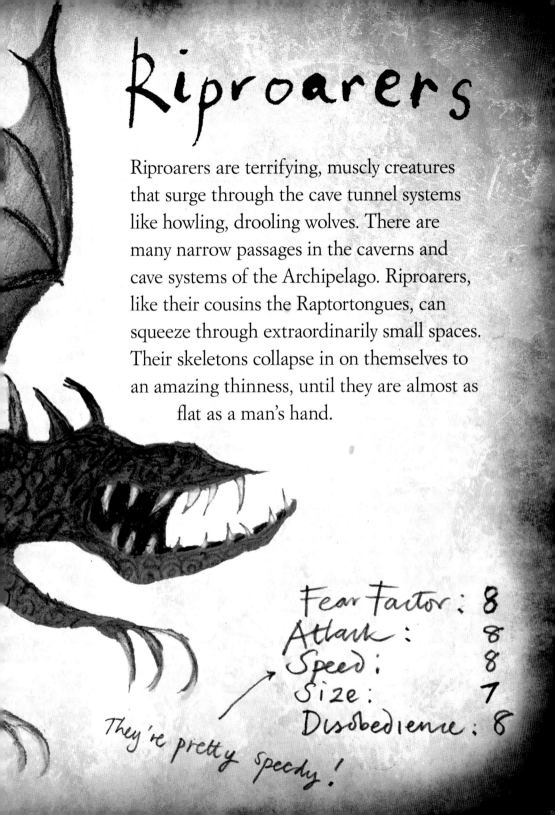

Riproarers

Riproarers are terrifying, muscly creatures that surge through the cave tunnel systems like howling, drooling wolves. There are many narrow passages in the caverns and cave systems of the Archipelago. Riproarers, like their cousins the Raptortongues, can squeeze through extraordinarily small spaces. Their skeletons collapse in on themselves to an amazing thinness, until they are almost as flat as a man's hand.

Fear Factor: 8
Attack: 8
Speed: 8
Size: 7
Disobedience: 8

They're pretty speedy!

Baby Riproarer

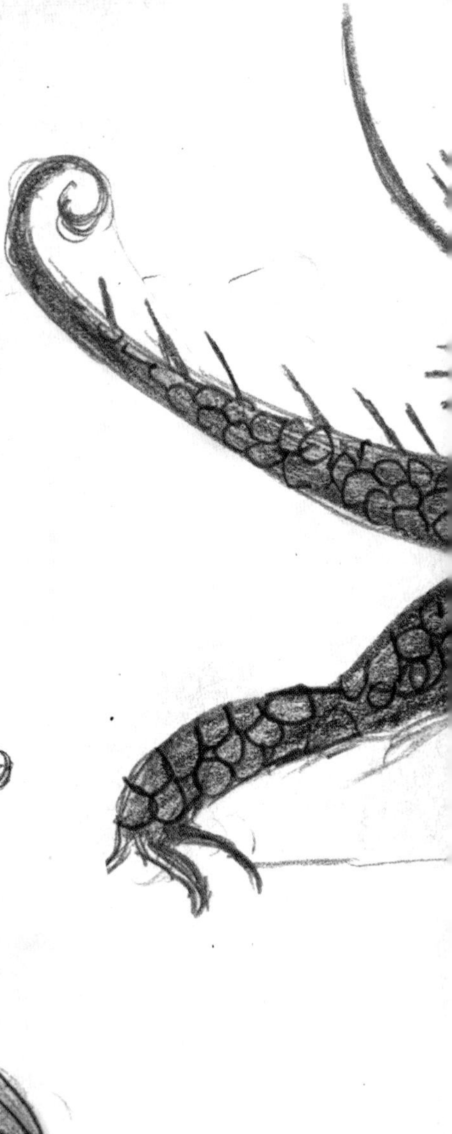

As with so many
baby dragons, even
the very scary ones
are extremely sweet...

Baby Riproarer
practicing
going flat

The head of a Riproarer, sliding, collapses completely flat, the bones can fit over one another, so the dragon through small openings.

A young Riproarer squeezing through a sudden narrowing of a cave tunnel.

Stickyworms

Fear Factor: 6 **Size:** 6
Attack: 6 **Disobedience:** 6
Speed: 3

A Stickyworm is twice the size of a boa constrictor.
They make Stickyworm webs from their saliva to
trap victims. Like slugs, Stickyworms react badly
to salt, so even a mere sprinkling of salt will stop
them in their tracks.

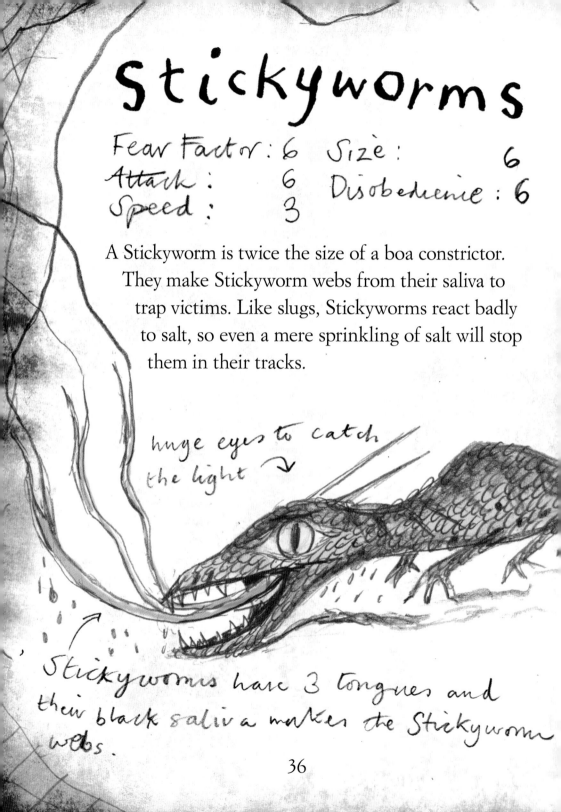

huge eyes to catch
the light

Stickyworms have 3 tongues and
their black saliva makes the Stickyworm
webs.

An unfortunate Viking

These strange lumps
are the Stickyworm's
latest meal

Lots and lots of feet

Stickyworms don't like
SALT, it stings their bodies
like an acid.

Driller-Dragons

Fear Factor: 8
Attack: 9
Speed: 6
Size: 6
Disobedience: 6

Driller-Dragons have drills on the end of their noses that they can revolve at amazing speed.

Skullions

Fear Factor: 9   Size: 7

Attack: 9

Speed: 9   Disobedience: 9

The Skullion is a rare, savage species of flightless dragon. Despite being blind and very nearly deaf, it is a fearsome predator, hunting in packs using a highly developed sense of smell alone. It has one extra-long super-sharp claw with which it disables its victims by cutting the Achilles tendon at the back of their heels, leaving them unable to walk. It then eats them alive.

Fear Factor: 8
Attack: 8
Speed: 2
Size: 8
Disobedience. 9

Strangulators

Monstrous Strangulators never see daylight
and are the colour of nothing. Their bodies
are transparent, so you can see the unfortunate
forms of dragons they have eaten moving through
their digestive systems. Strangulators can strangle
you to death with one of their tentacles. But in a
touch of evolutionary over-kill, they also have a
tail filled to the tip with venom, green as glass.
If you are injected with that poison, it is
goodbye, sweet world; hello, Valhalla.

Monstrous Strangulators are very heavily armed,
but they are not particularly intelligent, so it is
possible to trick them – if you get
the chance.

NESTING SITES

Some Viking Tribes steal their dragons as infants.
But many others steal their dragons as eggs from
the ancient wildwoods of the Barbaric Archipelago.
These wildwoods are home to adorable Shortwing
Squirrelserpents, chattering cheerily to each other as
they swing through the branches on their long stripy
tails, and cruel fat Breathquenchers who slide through
the tangles of the undergrowth, like illuminated pythons.

Night falls, and drifts of moth-like Scarers flutter out of
the way as packs of hungry Wolf-fangs use their night-
time vision to chase after the glowing body-heat of the
Cuckoo Dragons, and way up in the tiniest twigs of the
forest canopy, the Vampire Spydragons
eyes are watching…

Vampire Dragons

Fear Factor: 7
Attack: 7
Speed: 4
Size: 2
Disobedience: 9

The nocturnal blood-sucking Vampire Dragon anaesthetises its victim's skin before it bites.

Shortwing Squirrelserpent

Lively, chirpy little creatures, Shortwings have very long tails that end in a 'hook' so that they can get a better grip as they swing through the trees.

Fear Factor: 3
Attack: 2
Speed: 8
Size: 3
Disobedience: 8

Fear Factor: 3
Attack: 2
Speed: 4
Size: 6
Disobedience: 5

CUCKOO DRAGONS

The Cuckoo Dragon lays its
eggs in the nest of a bird, who then brings
up the infant dragon as if it were their own
baby, despite the growing size and strength
of the imposter. Rather sweetly, though, the
grown-up Cuckoo Dragon treats the adoptive
bird-parents with great love and affection,
and protects them ever after.

Firestarters

Fear Factor: 4
Attack: 4
Speed: 7
Size: 2
Disobedience: 7

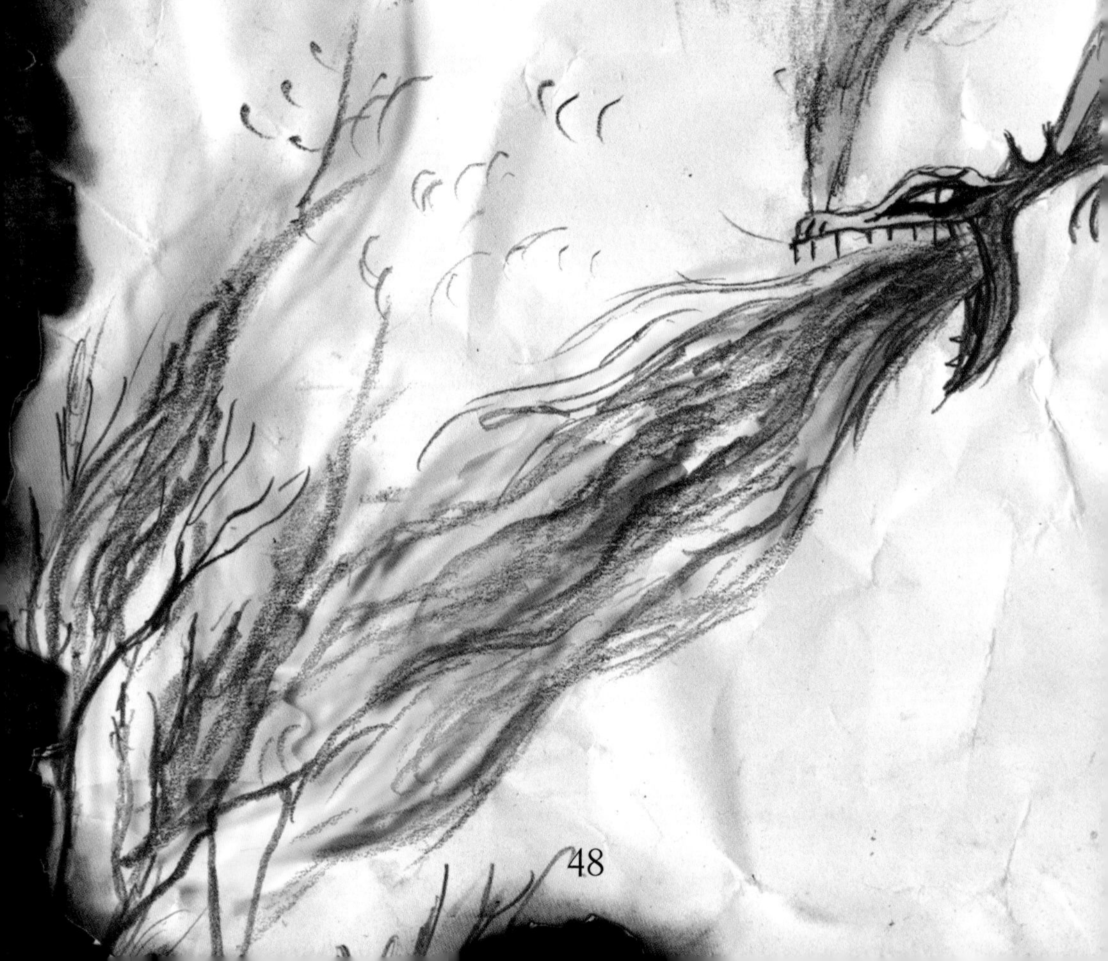

Fire Starters live in the Flaming Forest. Most dragons are careful not to set fire to the environment in which they live. Fire Starters need their eggs to incubate in fire so they constantly set fire to the forest. The forest only survives because it is also home to Water Dragons that put out the fires when they threaten to burn out of control.

Fear Factor: 4
Attack: 2
Speed: 4
Size: 8
Disobedience: 6

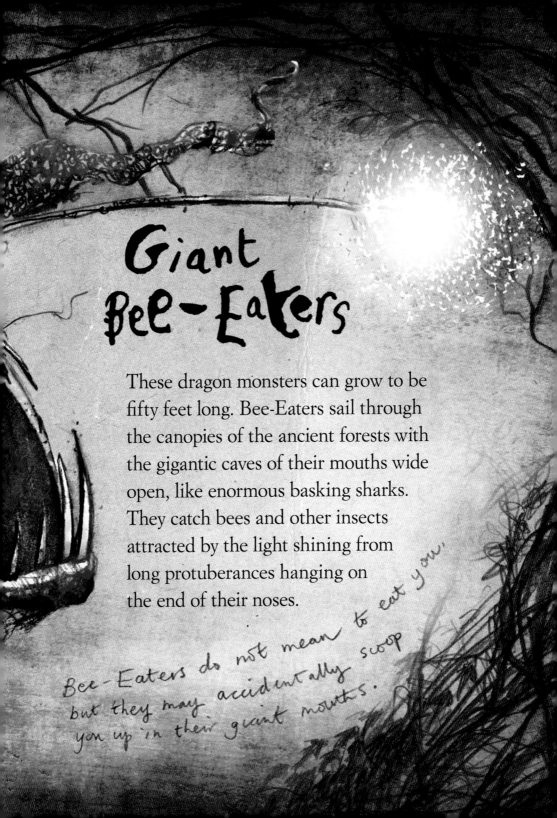

Giant Bee-Eaters

These dragon monsters can grow to be fifty feet long. Bee-Eaters sail through the canopies of the ancient forests with the gigantic caves of their mouths wide open, like enormous basking sharks. They catch bees and other insects attracted by the light shining from long protuberances hanging on the end of their noses.

Bee-Eaters do not mean to eat you, but they may accidentally scoop you up in their giant mouths.

Vampire Spydragons

Fear Factor: 8
Attack: 9
Speed: 5
Size: 7
Disobedience

Vampire Spydragons are chameleons that can turn invisible apart from their red eyes. When they bite a victim, they leave one of their teeth inside the wound, and use that tooth as a primitive tracking device.

I'm kind of just hoping a Spydragon will never bite me...

scarers!

Fear Factor: 9
Attack: 7
Speed: 7
Size: 2
Disobedience 9

Scarers feed on the
adrenalin caused by fear, so
they scare you nearly to death
before they bite you.

It is important to remain calm
when confronted by a swarm of scarers,
because if they do not smell fear,
they may not sense your presence.

Fear Factor : 5
Attack : 5
Speed : 7
Size : 4
Disobedience : 6

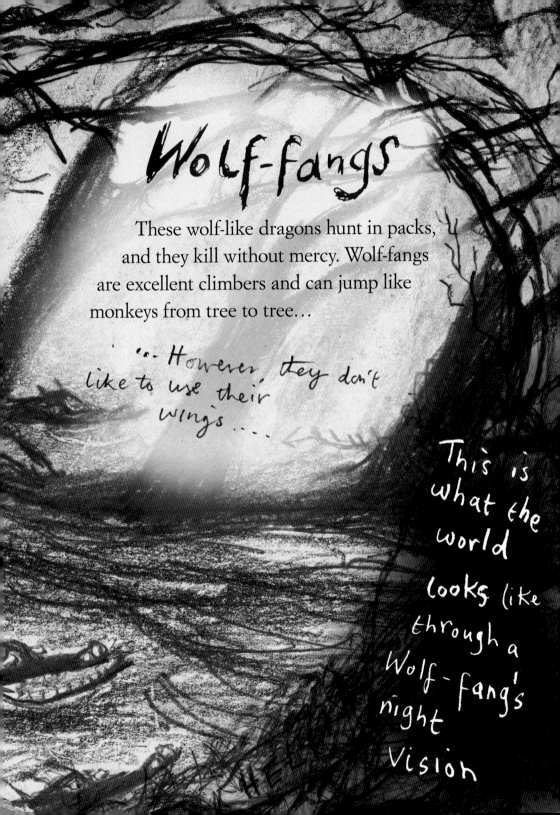

Wolf-fangs

These wolf-like dragons hunt in packs, and they kill without mercy. Wolf-fangs are excellent climbers and can jump like monkeys from tree to tree...

...However, they don't like to use their wings....

This is what the world looks like through a Wolf-fang's night vision

Fear Factor: 6
Attack: 6
Speed: 5
Size: 6
Disobedience: 7

Breathquenchers

Breathquenchers slide elegantly through the undergrowth and up the trees, as silent as a mist. Fully grown, they are at least twenty feet long and make even the largest python look like an earthworm. They wrap their coils around their victim and squeeze them slowly to death. Breathquenchers can dislocate their jaws to swallow an entire Bee-Eater whole and then spend the next three weeks sleeping in order to digest their meal. Breathquenchers are extremely intelligent, but their weakness is their vanity. If you carry a mirror with you, they can be sufficiently distracted by the vision of their own beauty to relax their coils and allow you to escape.

DRAGON EGGS

Vikings who survive the trip to the nesting-sites of the wildwoods and return home with a dragon egg have to be very certain that they can identify exactly what kind of species will hatch out of that egg. Dragon eggs are a little like mushrooms. Deadly Cap mushrooms look like normal field mushrooms and they taste rather pleasant. However, eating even 1 oz of a Deadly Cap mushroom is enough to kill you stone dead.

In the same way, a Common-or-Garden Dragon egg looks horribly similar to the egg of a Goreslingus Rex Dragon. But a baby Common-or-Garden Dragon is likely to lick you and think you are its mama, while a baby Goreslingus Rex Dragon will send you straight to Valhalla with one snort of its dear little nostrils. (Don't blame the poor baby Goreslingus Rex. It thinks it's being friendly.)

Both with mushrooms, and dragon eggs, it is generally a really bad idea if they glow in the dark . . .

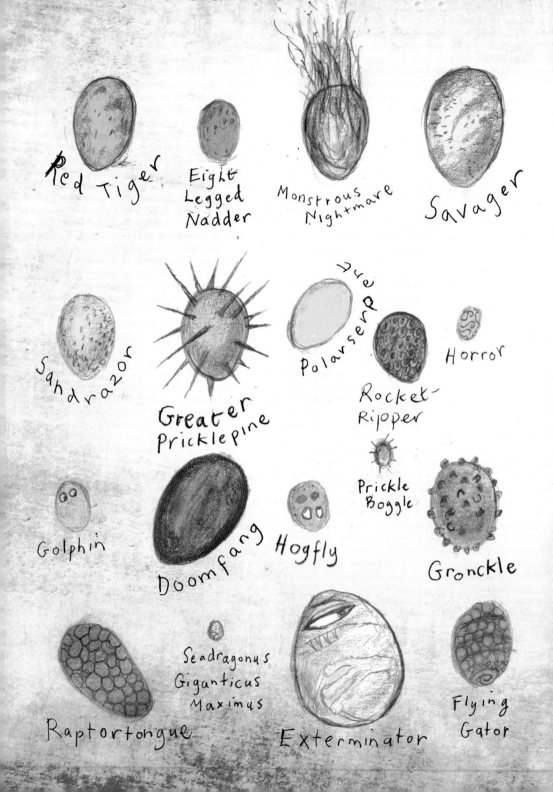

Rhinoback

Deadly
Shadow
Dragon

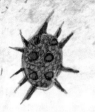

Devilish
Pervish

Driller-
Dragon

Sticky
Stealers

Long-
Eared
Flutterfire

Grimler

Marsh
Tiger

'X' dragon

Underground
Tail - hunter

Tiddly-Nip
Tick - Botherer

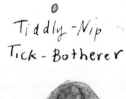

Windwalker

Winter
Flesher

Centidile

Breathquencher

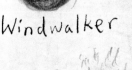

Toxic
Nightshade

DRAGON EGGS
and CHICKEN EGGS - NOT THE SAME.

Chicken eggs are small and white and defenceless and they don't move. You can easily put one in your pocket and it won't burst into flames.

The only thing that will hatch out of a chicken egg is a baby chick, and these are sweet and yellow and fluffy, and about as scary as a BUTTERCUP.

Dragon Egg.

chicken Egg

... Spot the Difference......

Dragon eggs are often heavily armed, and many of them move with frightening speed and DEADLY accuracy. The egg is so well equipped with egg defences it does not need to be guarded. NEVER put one in your pocket. The eggs can explode, shoot lightning bolts, or poisonous gases.

See what I mean?

NOT THE SAME

Eggs can
hide...

Squealer eggs
look like
rabbits'
droppings, but
with a long
nail
here

Eggs can
fly...

Golphin
Eggs
BOUNCE...

wheeeeee

Most dragons leave their eggs unattended for long periods of time. So the eggs have developed an astonishing number of interesting defences to avoid being eaten.

Eggs can be spiky, lumpy and in other ways difficult to swallow. They can be deadly poisonous. Others might be slimy or foul tasting or a revoltingly spongy texture. Eggs can give electric shocks, or leave the tongue full of prickles.

Doldrum eggs are as dark and heavy as lead, so even when freshly laid they are difficult to lift. They get denser and denser as the dragon incubates inside, sinking lower and lower into the ground, until by the time the egg hatches, the infant dragon is born at the bottom of a deep well.

Golphin eggs can leap to the height of the roof of a house. It is quite common, in spring, to see a pack of furious Sidewinders, trying to catch a marsh full of leaping Golphin eggs, merrily bouncing out of the way.

EGG DEFENCES

Eggs may be **SPIKY**...

or lumpy...

...or just plain **YUCKY.**

Many eggs have transparent shells... so if the foetal dragon spots a predator.

Some eggs **EXPLODE** as soon as you touch them.

(the egg has a double lining so the baby inside is safe.)

...the egg rolls, at great speed, out of the way...

If you happen to find some eggs whose parents have died...

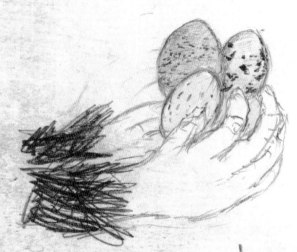

Take the orphan eggs very gently home...

...and put them in a warm fire.

Roll the egg into the fire, and wait. Eventually the egg
itself will burst into flames. It will begin to shake and
steam and turn darker in colour. As the egg cracks,
great shafts of lightning will burst through those cracks,
setting fire to all it touches with bright orange flames,
until finally…

... the egg explodes...

This is not a good moment for your dad to come back in the room, as it makes a tiny bit of a mess, and if you are really unlucky, the chairs will be on fire, and there will be dragon goo in his beard. This may get you in trouble.

The Chiefly
Hut of Stoick
the Vast, where
I grew up.

DOMESTIC DRAGONS

Dragons that we take from the wild and turn into
hunting-dragons or riding-dragons, are called domestic
dragons. Most hunting-dragons are likely to be of the
BOG DRAGON species. On the outskirts of Viking
villages, you can see the yellow eyes of Flying Gators as
they lurk in the depths of the bog and the curl and rattle
of a slinking Sidewinder, slipping through the bracken,
fleeing the Flashfangs.

The little
hut in the bog
where Fishlegs lives,
all alone with the
Long-Eared Caretaker
dragon.
(it is slowly sinking)

BOG DRAGONS

The Common-or-Garden or Basic Brown

Fear Factor: 3
Attack: 3
Speed: 4
Size: 4
Disobedience: 1

The Common-or-Garden and the Basic Brown are poor hunters, but easy to train. These dragons are the best kind for family pets. I believed that Toothless was a Common-or-Garden when I first got him.

Flashfangs

Fear Factor: 3

Attack: 3

Speed: 7

Size: 3

Disobedience: 6

Lithe little black panther-like creatures, a little smaller than a wolf. Too large to be hunting-dragons, too small to be riding-dragons, and curiously un-trainable, Flashfangs are a real pest to the Vikings. They snatch Viking deer, they kill Viking sheep, and so every now and then, the Viking Tribes go on a Flashfang hunt to keep down the numbers of these 'vermin'.

Flying Gators

These dragons are related very closely to alligators and crocodiles. Many goggles of Gators can be found in the soggy bogs of the Haunted Marshes. They lie, silently submerged up to their eyeballs in the mud, so that they can launch a surprise attack on an infant Marsh Tiger, or a baby Gloomer.

Gators are extremely stupid, so if you are attacked by one, imitate the ticking noise of a Toxic Nightshade, and it will immediately release you and swim away through the bog, despite the fact that human beings are WAY too large to be confused with a Toxic Nightshade...

Fear Factor: 6

Attack: 4

Speed: 5

Size: 4

Disobedience: 7

Rhino backs

Fear Factor: 7   Size: 8
Attack: 7   Disobedience: 8
Speed: 5

Rhinobacks are aggressive carnivores and will
attack human towns and villages out of pure spite,
as well as for food. Gormlesses are vegetarian,
feeding slowly and happily on vast areas of
wood and forest.

Rhinobacks don't like the smell
of CHEESE.

BIG SPOTTED GORMLESS

Gormlesses are way too lazy to breed, so there are not that many of them.

Although Gormlesses are very good-natured, they are also short-sighted, so they will often accidentally sit on a village, not realising it is there.

Fear Factor : 3
Attack : 3
Speed : 1
Size : 8
Disobedience : 7

81

Sidewinders

Sidewinders are chameleons, about the size of small cats. They hunt in packs and perform hypnotizing dances to confuse their victims. Sidewinders are hunted by many other dragons, so they have extra eyes, camouflage and a wiggling, sideways flying movement to evade attackers. The chameleon eggs of Sidewinders have small holes, through which the infant Sidewinder keeps an eye out for predators. If a predator approaches, the Sidewinder egg rolls rapidly to safety, hiding in a nearby tree stump or patch of flowers.

Fear Factor: 2
Attack: 4
Speed: 6
Size: 2
Disobedience: 6

The Monstrous Nightmare

Fear Factor: 3   Size: 3

Attack: 6   Disobedience: 3

Speed: 8

By unofficial Viking law only a Chief or the son of a Chief can own a Monstrous Nightmare.

(but of course, Snotlout has one anyway)

DRAGONFIGHT... between killer and FIREWORM

Gloomers

Fear Factor: 2   Size: 4
Attack: 2   Disobedience: 2
Speed: 3

Gloomers are prone to sadness and depression.
A Gloomer egg becomes so heavy over the course
of its incubation, that it sinks lower
and lower into the ground,
eventually forming a
deep well.

Trying
to cheer
up a baby
Gloomer
can be
tricky

Long-Eared Caretaker Dragon

Fear Factor: 3

Attack: 6

Speed: 4

Size: 5

Disobedience: 1

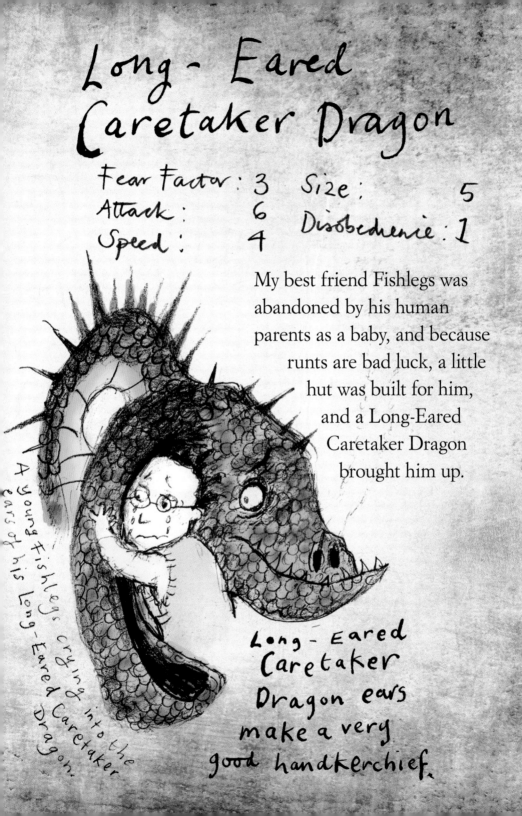

My best friend Fishlegs was abandoned by his human parents as a baby, and because runts are bad luck, a little hut was built for him, and a Long-Eared Caretaker Dragon brought him up.

A young Fishlegs crying into the ears of his Long-Eared Caretaker Dragon.

Long-Eared Caretaker Dragon ears make a very good handkerchief.

Long Eared Caretaker Dragon egg

Long Eared Caretaker Dragon egg

After she lays her eggs, the female Long-Eared Caretaker Dragon places them carefully inside the ears of the male where they will be warm and dry until they hatch.

Long-Eared Caretaker Dragons carry their babies in their ears

Learning to WALK

The baby Fishlegs learning to walk.

Learning to walk is hard for Long-Eared Caretaker Dragons because they are always accidentally tripping over their own ears...

hello!...

whoops...

OW!!

Fear Factor: 2
Attack: 2
Speed: 3
Size: 3
Disobedience: 6

webbed feet for swimming through Marshes

Marsh Tigers

Marsh Tigers are riding-dragons that live in the marshes in the wild. They have webbed feet and prominent noses so that they can breathe while wallowing in the mud. They are known as 'Tigers' because of the characteristic stripy pattern of their skin.

Marsh Tigers lay their eggs in little nests shaped like baskets, which drift like floating islands down the stream. The eggs are brightly coloured in a tiger pattern, to let other dragons know the eggs are highly poisonous.

Marsh Tigers have an unfortunate downside as riding-dragons. Whenever they see water, they submerge themselves up to their nostrils. Unless they can be trained out of this, it is very inconvenient for the rider.

Fear Factor: 9
Attack: 8
Speed: 7
Size: 2
Disobedience: 10

Poisonous Piffleworms

Poisonous Piffleworms cannot stand the sound of whistling, it freezes them still as statues.

Venomous Vorpents

Fear Factor: 9
Attack: 9
Speed: 8
Size: 1
Disobedience: 9

The only known antidote to Vorpent Venom is the Vegetable-That-No-One-Dares-Name (a potato), which can only be found in The-Land-That-Does-Not-Exist (America).

Arsenic Adderwings

Fear Factor: 9
Attack: 10
Speed: 2
Size: 1
Disobedience: 8

Arsenic Adderwings look exactly like Glow-worms, apart from the red spot in their tail. DO NOT TOUCH THEM. Arsenic Adderwings cannot stand the colour yellow (their only known predator is a Toxic Nightshade).

Toxic Nightshades

Fear Factor: 9
Attack: 10
Speed: 7
Size: 2
Disobedience: 9

Toxic Nightshades are yellow, and they make a loud ticking noise to warn unobservant dragons that it would be a Very Bad Mistake to try to eat them.

Tickling Nightshades behind the ears sends them into a trance and they won't attack.

Eight-Legged Battlegore

Fear Factor: 8
Attack: 9
Speed: 8
Size: 7
Disobedience: 6

Battlegores are amazingly speedy, considering how big they are.

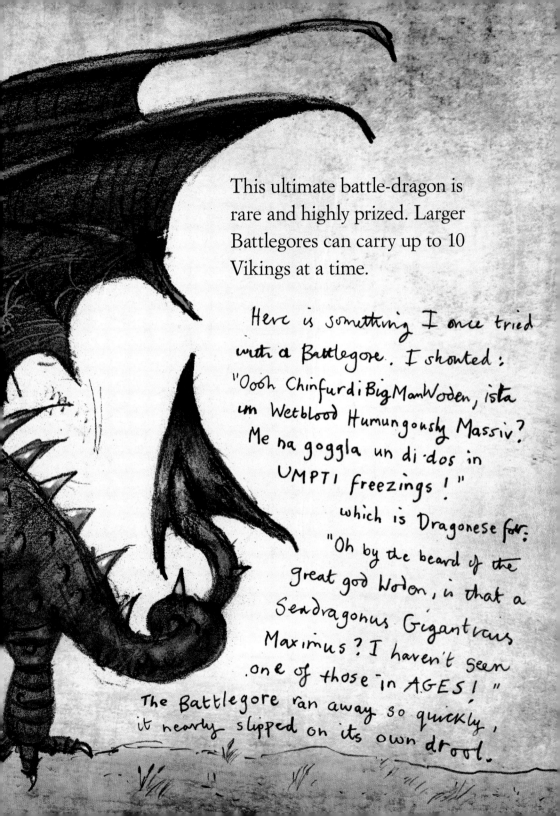

This ultimate battle-dragon is rare and highly prized. Larger Battlegores can carry up to 10 Vikings at a time.

Here is something I once tried with a Battlegore. I shouted:
"Oooh Chinfurdi BigManWoden, ista um Wetblood Humungously Massiv? Me na goggla un di dos in UMPTI freezings!"

which is Dragonese for:
"Oh by the beard of the Great god Woden, is that a Sendragonus Gigantiaus Maximus? I haven't seen one of those in AGES!"

The Battlegore ran away so quickly, it nearly slipped on its own drool.

stink dragons

Fear Factor: 4   Size: 3
Attack: 7   Disobedience: 8
Speed: 3

A Stink Dragon's defence is very similar to a skunk's.
Disturb it, or make it feel as if it is in danger and it
will open its mouth and spray out a stinky mist
that drenches its victim. If a Stink
Dragon 'stinks' you,
nobody will come near
you for at least a week.
Indeed, for the first 48 hours the
smell is so indescribably awful that it is
almost physically impossible to approach you.

Hypnomunks

Fear Factor: 4
Attack: 5
Speed: 7
Size: 2
Disobedience: 6

Hypnomunks are cute little creatures slightly larger than a domestic cat or a weasel. They catch their prey through the power of their hypnotic gaze, and an extraordinary rhythmic chant that interrupts the radar and echolocation skills of smaller dragons. A spell of Hypnomunks, working together by chanting and clicking, can make a Scarer or a Ravenhunter literally fall out of the sky, unconscious.

DON'T LOOK INTO THEIR EYES

Squealers

AAAl!

Fear Factor: 3
Attack: 3
Speed: 1
Size: 2
Disobedience: 5

Squealer eggs are
EXACTLY the same size,
shape, and consistency
as rabbit droppings,
(I'm sorry, but it's true)
except they already
have that extra-long
nail growing out the top.

Squealers are blobby, slug-like creatures. They have no legs to chase after their prey, so they lie on their backs waving their extra-long nails gently in the air. Any animal that comes into contact with those nails causes the whole pack of Squealers to scream unbearably loudly. The scream is so loud it can kill smaller dragons stone dead on the spot. The Squealers then devour their victim, slithering all over it like revolting slug-like jellyfish.

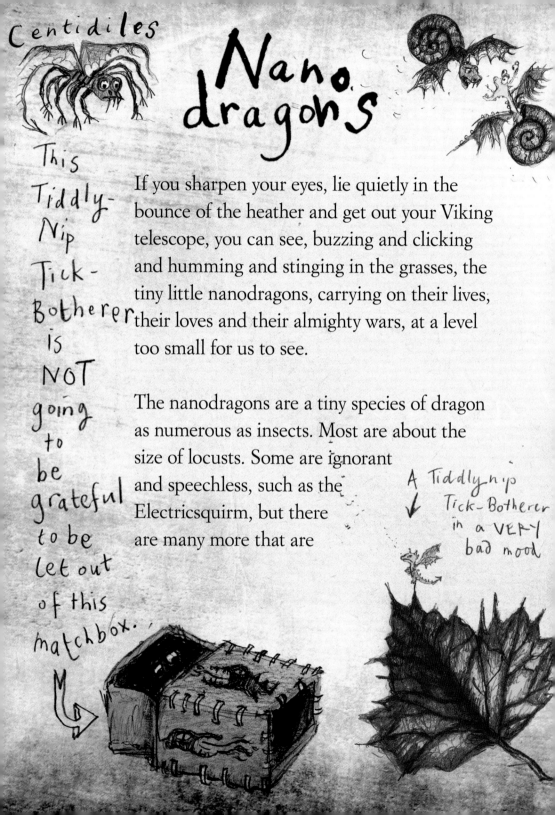

Centidiles

Nano dragons

This Tiddly-Nip Tick-Botherer is NOT going to be grateful to be let out of this matchbox.

If you sharpen your eyes, lie quietly in the bounce of the heather and get out your Viking telescope, you can see, buzzing and clicking and humming and stinging in the grasses, the tiny little nanodragons, carrying on their lives, their loves and their almighty wars, at a level too small for us to see.

The nanodragons are a tiny species of dragon as numerous as insects. Most are about the size of locusts. Some are ignorant and speechless, such as the Electricsquirm, but there are many more that are

A Tiddly-nip Tick-Botherer in a VERY bad mood

Plankenteenies

Not Real Size →

Real Size ↙

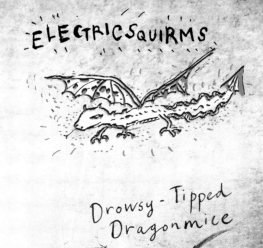

ELECTRICSQUIRMS

Drowsy-Tipped Dragonmice

intelligent and organised, despite
their small size. Even though they
are often too small to see, the whole
of the Archipelago is alive with
nanodragons, hopping through
the heather, ticking in the grasses,
bowling like dust upon the wind.

Flutterfires

PRICKLEBOGGLES

Drowsy-Tipped Dragonmice

Dragonmice are very sweet indeed, but they sleep for nearly 23 3/4 hours per day. For the quarter of an hour that they are awake, they are extraordinarily active, because they need to get a lot done in a very short space of time, so they move at speeds impossible to see with the human eye. In 15 minutes of blurry activity, they track down their prey, kill it and eat it. Then they fall asleep again.

PRICKLEBOGGLES

Prickleboggles are so very, very stupid. This one can't remember, does he eat the ant or does the ant eat him?

Flutterfires

Flutterfires are gorgeous little nanodragons that look very like butterflies. They are addicted to the nectar of flowers which can send them into a catnip frenzy. The meadows and heathers of the Archipelago hum with the drowsy, drunken Flutterfires, stumbling, intoxicated, from one flower to another, trailing little clouds of smoke behind them. Flutterfires don't only exist on flower nectar, though. They use their fire to barbecue ants and bumblebees, and other smaller insects.

ELECTRICSQUIRMS

Fig 1:
The RIGHT WAY to
hold an Electricsquirm,
BY THE
TAIL.

Fig 2: →
The WRONG
WAY to hold
an
Electricsquirm

1. Toothless p-p-promised Hiccup he would never eat strange eggs again. Toothless will be GOOD.

2. But they're BLUE ones, Toothless loves blue ones...

Hmmm

3.

4. WRONG DECISION.

G-G-U-L-P.

Ziggerastica

Emperor Beetleboog
BOLDERBUGS

The king of the nanodragons is always a very special
species of nanodragon called an Emperor Beetleboog
Bolderbug. These ladybird-like little creatures,
with glossy red bodies and handsome black spots,
live considerably longer than most nanodragons. A
Flutterfire only lives for a couple of years. But an
Emperor Beetleboog Bolderbug can live for decades.
Ziggerastica is the present king of the nanodragons, and
he is dangerous only because he commands so many
millions of nanodragons, that if he were to side with the

Dragon Furious, the humans would be doomed. Luckily Ziggerastica doesn't really consider the War to be any of his business. Ziggerastica is under the impression that he is the Living God, the most Important Being in the Galaxy. He believes that the moon shines and the sun rises only to light the way and warm the wings of Ziggerastica the Emperor Beetleboog Bolderbug. Don't laugh too loudly at him. There are humans who suffer from the same delusion.

Ziggerastica has a weakness, and that is honey. He loves the stuff.

"I am Ziggerastica, the Living God, most high despot of the northern grasses".

↓

Fear Factor: 8
Attack: 9
Speed: 4
Size: 1
Disobedience: 10

TRAINING YOUR HUNTING OR LAP-DRAGON

Training your dragon, means teaching them who is the Boss. The traditional Viking method for training dragons is YELLING at them. But your hunting-dragons and riding-dragons will be by your side in battle for the rest of your life. If you have trained them through fear, will they come to your rescue in a life-threatening situation?

Training your dragon without fear is definitely the Hard Way to train your dragon. It needs careful study of Dragonese, the language that dragons speak to one another, which is complicated for humans to speak, because we do not have forked tongues. It also takes a great deal of patience, because your dragon will not necessarily do what it is told the first time. Or, indeed, the two hundred and first time…

Interestingly, it is the cutest and smallest hunting-dragons and lap-dragons that are the most obstinate and the hardest to train.

The Cuties

Hogflys

Aunt Gladioli of the Monobrow, and her Puggles, Crusher, Bloodspot and Tinkle. (they BITE.)

Horrors

pricklepines

Puggles

Aunt Burlysweet's
Specklebound and
her five babies,

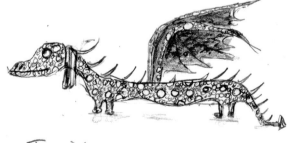

... and Niff

Twiglet,
Spicklet,
Joglet
Piggerwrigglet...

109

The Aunts and Their Dragon

Aunt Egginbreeza Six-Pints
and her Bullpuff,
    Crashbark ⟿

Toothless is the NAUGHTIEST dragon in the Archiplego

oh
strike

I have to admit, that Toothless, my hunting-dragon, is one of the naughtiest dragons in the Archipelago. He poos in my father's slippers… He goes on strike… He will not go to bed on time… He bites people on the nose… Young dragons do not always know what is good for them.

However, because I can speak to Toothless in the language of Dragonese, I don't have to yell at him, I can be cunning. I can bribe him to eat up his wood by telling him jokes…

doing a poo in Alvin's helmet

Here he is, pooing in my father's slippers

STOICK

JOKES

The only way I have ever managed to train Toothless is by bribing him with telling him jokes

How do you know when a Seadragonus Giganticus Maximus is under your bed??

When your nose hits the ceiling...

HAHA HA H-HA HA

What do you find inside Wartihog's clean nose? Fingerprints.

What's the best way to catch a Basic Brown?

Have someone throw it at you.

HA HA HA HA HA

Sometimes Toothless is laughing so HARD he forgets to fly and then he falls out of the sky. tee-hee

what dragon can jump higher than the Great Hall?

Great Halls can't jump.

Are you all right, Toothless?

The human tongue is not forked so speaking Dragonese can get tricky

Speaking Dragonese

Here is an example of Toothless talking to me in Dragonese, with the Norse translation below.

Me has b-b-buckets ði belly-scream
I am very hungry

Me isna burped si Issa midðling o ði zuzztime
I don't care if it IS the middle of the night

Me has o-o-o-opla ði larði-gurgles
My tummy is rumbling like anything

Plus me needy ði grubbings SNIP-SNAP!
And I want food RIGHT NOW!

Oo mes'll ðo ði yowlyshreekers too fortissimo
theys'll earwig me inði BigManGaff
Or I'll scream so loudly they'll hear me in Valhalla

Plus yow pappa issa z-z-zzuzzing indi hovel ensweet
And your dad is sleeping in the room next door

Me coglet hissa peepers undo
I think he might wake up

Plus hes'll do di heeby-jeebies
And he won't be very pleased

Me needy di S-S-S-S-SALTSICKS
I want OYSTERS

Me isna burped si issa middling o di zuzztime
I don't care if it is the middle of the night

Yow g-g-grabba di saltsicks low indi landscoop
You can get oysters from the harbour

Sna staraway
It's not far

M-M-Me gogo ta yowlshreek...
I'm starting to scream...

(three quarters of an hour later)

Yow me p-p-peepers undo!
You woke me up!

Wah is DA?
What is THAT?

Da na goggle com s-s-saltsicks...
That doesn't look like oysters...

DA goggle com sniffersludge...
THAT looks like bogeys...

Sniffersludge p-p-plus di squidink tiddles...
Bogeys with black bits in them...

Me no likeit di squidink tiddles
I don't like black bits

Issa y-y-yuck-yuck
They're disgusting

Watever, me is tow zuzzready por di scrumming
Anyway, I'm too tired to eat

Mes'll zip di peepers
I'm going to sleep

Yow thunderpuffs issa zapping
You're in a very bad mood (literally, your stormclouds
are crackling)

P-P-Poor
Toothless
is
S-S-starving

STOP
Copying
me, Toothless!

The only problem with learning to communicate with your dragon, of course, is that they can communicate back…

ME: (despairingly)
Please eat up your firewood!

TOOTHLESS: Please eat up your firewood!

ME: Don't start this now, Toothless, you know it drives me crazy...

TOOTHLESS: Don't start this now, Toothless, you know it drives me crazy...

ME (cross): Stop copying me!

TOOTHLESS (delighted):
S-s-stop copying me!

S-s-stop
copying me,
Toothless!

120

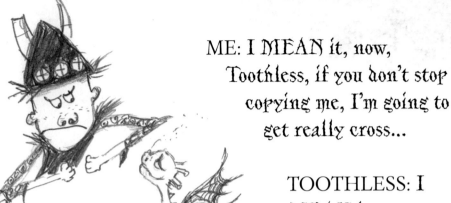

ME: I MEAN it, now, Toothless, if you don't stop copying me, I'm going to get really cross...

TOOTHLESS: I MEAN it now, T-t-toothless, if you don't stop copying me, I'm going to get really cross...

I stomp round the room tearing my hair out.

ME (yelling): STOP COPYING ME!

TOOTHLESS (yelling): STOP COPYING ME!

STOP. copying Me!!

121

ME: EEEAARRGH!!!!!!

TOOTHLESS: EEEEARRRGGH!!!!!!

I run from the room.

STOP
C-C-COPYING
ME!!

EEeeargh....

TOOTHLESS
is THE BOSS.

Hunting-dragons can be unbelievably selfish and disobedient. At times they will drive you crazy, demanding oysters at two o'clock in the morning, for example, or having a tantrum in front of the entire assembled Tribes of the Archipelago in the middle of the quietest and most solemn moment of the Winter Solstice Ceremony.

But trust me, if you train your dragon the Hard Way, you will develop an unshakeable and lifelong bond…

Eventually.

These are
Toothless's real
footprints I'm afraid

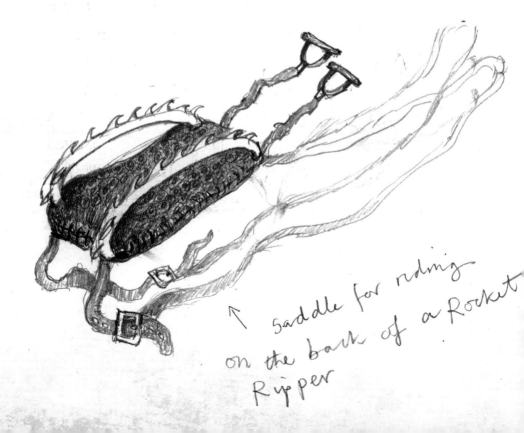

saddle for riding
on the back of a Rocket
Ripper

DRAGON RIDING

Once young Vikings have trained (or tried to train) their hunting-dragons, the next step in a Warrior's Initiation is to learn to fly their riding-dragon. There is no experience on earth like the sheer heart-thumping, head-spinning, joy of flying on the back of a dragon...

Riding-dragons are generally taken from the Sky Dragon species. Faster than falcons and slicker than witches, the Dervishes curl gloriously through the cloud and thunderstorms, and wheeling by their side, slaloming sinuously through the jutting rocks of the islands, as neat as threading a needle, are the Tornados and the Rocket Rippers, and the odd rare glimpse of a diving Phantom.

Sky Dragons

Here, Hiccup the First is sitting on the back of a very rare female Silver Phantom (only the females have that single horn like a unicorn)

Silver Phantoms

Fear Factor 10
Attack 10
Speed 10
Size 7
Disobedience ... 8

Chickenpoxers

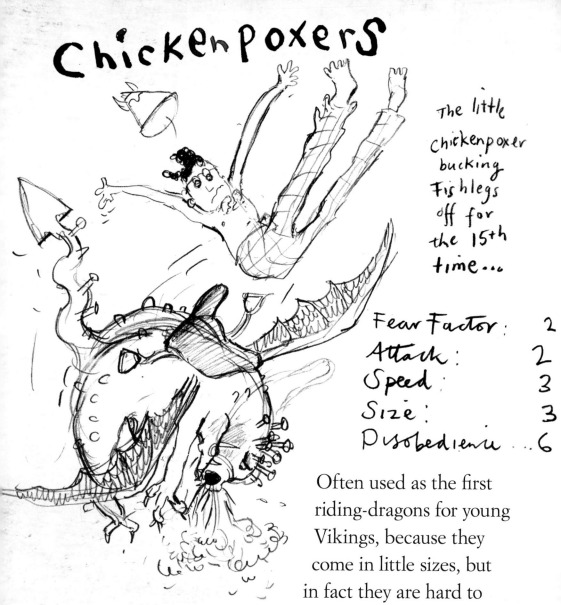

The little chickenpoxer bucking Fishlegs off for the 15th time...

Fear Factor: 2
Attack: 2
Speed: 3
Size: 3
Disobedience ...6

Often used as the first riding-dragons for young Vikings, because they come in little sizes, but in fact they are hard to ride because they are so hot-tempered. They often stop suddenly in mid-air so the rider sails over the dragon's head, or buck madly, like a wild horse, unseating the rider in seconds.

Two-Headed Gormatron

Fear Factor: 2 Size: 4
Attack: 1 Disobedience: 6
Speed: 2

Gormatrons are so stupid, that it is truly remarkable that they have survived in the Barbaric Archipelago. Perhaps it is because they are a bit smelly and don't taste very nice. The two heads often pull the Gormatron in opposite directions, causing it to go round in circles, sometimes for hours. And by the time it has stopped going round in circles, it has forgotten what it was doing in the first place.

The ultimate battle dragon, most Viking warriors have a riding-dragon that is a Bullrougher. These tough dragons are surprisingly nimble in the air considering their size, weight and body armour.

BULLROUGHERS

Fear Factor : 5
Attack : 7
Speed : 7
Size : 7
Disobedience : 4

Rocket Rippers

Fear Factor: 7 Size: 6
Attack: 7 Disobedience: 6
Speed: 9

Rocket Rippers have awesome flying skills.
They are completely flat so the rider has to
lie on his or her stomach which makes
them tricky to control.

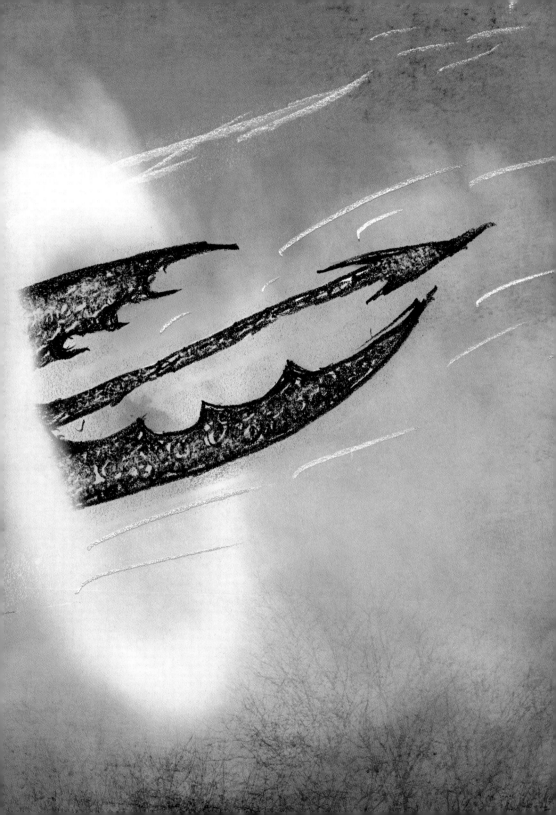

Zebramounts

Fear Factor: 1

Attack: 1

Speed: 1

Size: 3

Disobedience: 4

A Zebramount is often a first choice of riding-dragon for a young Viking, because of their gentle, placid natures. However, it can be difficult to get them moving at all.

Ravenhunters

Fear Factor: 3   Size: 2
Attack: 2   Disobedience: 3
Speed: 8

Ravenhunters are used by Alvin the Treacherous as
spy dragons, or to carry messages. These dragons are
immensely greedy, so they can be bribed to change sides,
if they are offered sufficient quantities of their favourite
food, scallops.

Here, Snotlout's little sister, Adelaide, is demonstrating the importance of the safety strap

LEARNING to RIDE

Riding-dragons come in all shapes and sizes. The first ride for a lot of young Vikings is something very slow or very small, like a Zebramount or a Chickenpoxer. Chickenpoxers can be rather bad-tempered.

Here, Snotlout's little sister Adelaide is demonstrating how important it is to have a safety strap. The safety strap attaches the ankle to the saddle, and means that if the rider falls off in the air, he or she dangles from underneath the dragon's stomach until the dragon manages to make an emergency landing, or the rider hauls him or herself back into the saddle.

You will fall off your dragon many, many times before you learn how to balance yourself properly. DO NOT GIVE UP.

Camicazi riding her Rocket Ripper, Typhoon,
very low over the Murderous Mountains

← Snotlout showing off

Once you have mastered the basics, dragons can be ridden in various different ways. The extreme flatness of Rocket Rippers makes them exceptionally fast and aerodynamic, and excellent for low flying over enemy territory. But the rider has to lie on their stomach, as if they were riding a sled or toboggan.

Only a very skilled Dragon Rider indeed has the balance and the control for the Flashburn Stand-Up position.

Snotlout's riding-dragon, a Devilish Derrick, is very difficult to control, but extremely quick and daring.

Here are various tricky riding techniques:

THE SWIVELS

Good for slaloming through the pointy peaks of gorges, or low flying mountains. A single mistake when doing the swivels can end in disaster.

LOOP THE LOOPS

The Dragon Rider needs exceptionally strong knees for this one, because the dragon turns upside down, mid loop, and if the rider isn't careful he will find himself hanging from the safety straps by his ankles, which is never a cool look.

SWITCH-LEAPS

These are particularly dangerous because the rider has to remove the safety strap mid-air to make the leap. In one of Grimbeard the Ghastly's greatest triumphs, way back in time, he Switch-leaped on to the back of an Uglithug king's dragon mid-battle, and threw the king down into the sea.

You can see from the pleased look on Camicazi's face that this is REALLY REALLY dangerous.

DRAGON EVOLUTION

a baby Windwalker

My own riding-dragon, a Windwalker, is an example of a dragon who 'evolves' during the course of its life-time. A newborn Windwalker is a rather extraordinary ball of feathers and fur, that looks remarkably like a cross-eyed duckling mixed with an anxious wolf cub.

A young Windwalker does not run or fly very fast. Its fur slows it down, and it has wobbly ankles, and bendy wings ...

146

As it grows, the Windwalker gradually sheds its hair, and becomes sleeker, faster and more aerodynamic. The ankles strengthen, the bending wings become an advantage as the dragon gains control and mastery over them, and by the time it reaches its late adolescence, the Windwalker is nearly as fast as the Silver Phantom. In its seventeenth year, the Windwalker enters its chrysalis stage…

a Windwalker chrysalis

Like a great black butterfly, the Windwalker builds its chrysalis inside a dark remote cave. It stays inside the chrysalis for six or seven months…

… and I am not quite sure what will happen next, because my own Windwalker hasn't evolved yet…

TRUE FLYING

Once you really know how to dragon ride, you no longer need the saddle, the reins and the safety strap. Dragons are wild creatures, and they should not be saddled like horses or chained like dogs. Once upon a time, in the lost Kingdom of the Wilderwest, where the humans and dragons were equals, all the Dragon Riders rode bareback, for that is true dragon riding, that is pure flying.

I have flown so high on the back of my Windwalker that it feels as if his wing-tips are brushing the very moon itself… Up so high that my helmet touches the stars, and Windwalker's wings are my wings, and his heart is my heart.

That is true dragon riding… That is pure flying…

Fishlegs's riding-dragon, the Deadly Shadow, is highly prized for its camouflage and its lightning bolt firepower...

THE WILDER SPECIES

Fishlegs's riding-dragon, the Deadly Shadow, often thought to be a Sky Dragon is actually a Mountain Dragon. Some of the most highly prized hunting, driving and spy dragons come from the mountainous regions of the Archipelago, where the dragons are particularly wild and dangerous. But it is a brave Viking who dares enter mountain territory to try and train or ride these dragons, with their remarkable hunting and tracking skills, and their hatred of humans.

Razorwings spin through the dizzying drops and fearful peaks of the Murderous Mountains, hunted down by the Tongue-twisters, with their long muscly repellent tongues, and the Hellsteethers, whose second set of jaws launch out towards their victims, teeth snapping independently, like the chattering of a skeleton. But most remarkable of all are the Stealth Dragons and Deadly Shadows, so well camouflaged that they are virtually invisible, appearing out of nowhere with their quick sharp fangs and electric bolts of lightning, before melting back into the mountains, like visions from a nightmare…

MOUNTAIN DRAGONS

Razorwings

Fear Factor: 7 Size: 6
Attack: 7 Disobedience: 7
Speed: 7

These dragons have razor-sharp wings that can decapitate victims in a heartbeat. They can turn as flat as a spinning blade, and are armed with mildly poisonous darts.

hates fish

Raptortongues

Speed: 7
Fear Factor: 7   Size: 7
Attack: 7   Disobedience: 5

Raptortongues live hidden in the deep crevasses of the Murderous Mountains or the Gorge of the Thunderbolt of Thor. They have an extraordinary ability to flatten themselves, which means they can squeeze through surprisingly small paces. They make excellent spy dragons.

loves chicken

Exterminators

Fear Factor : 9   Size : 6

Attack : 9   Disobedience : 7

Speed : 9

You have to kill
Exterminators TWICE
before they die...

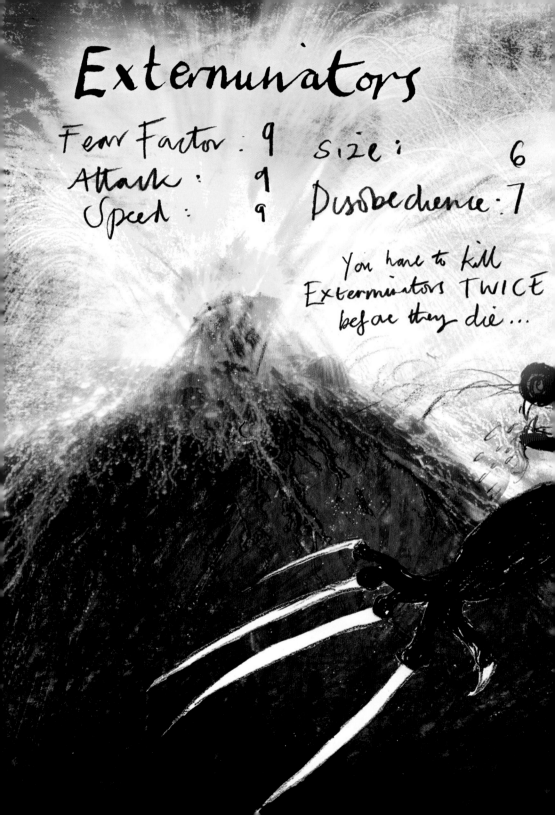

This Exterminator is being ridden by
my arch-enemy, Alvin the Treacherous,
a man who has now sworn to hunt all
dragons down to extinction.

Fear Factor: 8   Size: 5
Attack: 8   Disobedience: 9
Speed: 9

This Grimler dragon adopted Hiccup Horrendous
Haddock the Second when he was a baby. She was
able to do this because Grimlers suckle their young
like mammals. The Grimler went on to have a batch of
three young Grimlers of her own, and also later adopted
a lonely young Sea Dragon who befriended the young
Hiccup. The Sea Dragon grew up to become the
mighty Dragon FURIOUS.

Mood-Dragons

Fear Factor: 4
Attack: 6
Speed: 9
Size: 3
Disobedience: 7

A Mood-dragon changes colour according to its mood. It turns a deep blue-black when angry, orangey-pink when excited and a very pale green when nervous. Mood-dragons vary enormously in size. Some are as small as spaniels, others as big as a lioness.

Why, hello there, Toothless...

Babies?
What babies?
I'm a free spirit,
I don't have babies...

Mama!

stormgly
happy $\rightarrow$ jealous $\rightarrow$ angry

167

BULLGUARD
SLAVEDRAGONS

Fear Factor: 7
Attack: 7
Speed: 6
Size: 7
Disobedience: 4

A heavily armoured battle
dragon, with multiple eyes.

A bot of pepper is useful,
because it makes the
Slavedragon's eyes water

Snub-Nosed Hellsteethers

Fear Factor: 9 Size : 8
Attack : 9 Disobedience : 9
Speed : 8

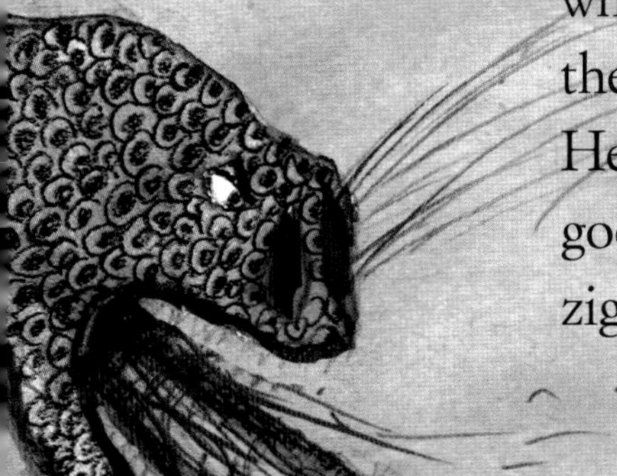

Hellsteethers have a second
pair of extendable jaws, with
which they reach out and grab
their victims, and they spit acid.
Hellsteether eyesight is not very
good so flying or running in a
zig-zag motion confuses them.

Hellsteethers have a weak spot —
unfortunately it is INSIDE their mouths...

DRAGON TRACKING

The mountain regions are dangerous, and if you want to track a particular dragon, or if you are in unfamiliar territory and want to know what kind of dragons might be around, a knowledge of the different types of dragon poos can come in handy. Yucky, but true.

A highly coloured dragon dropping often indicates a poisonous species.

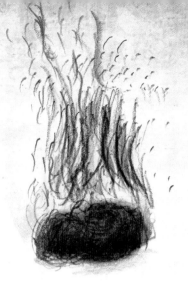

Stinkdragon

Marsh Tiger

Flying Gators

Glow-worm

Monstrous Nightmare poos are flaming, as are Firestarters, and many others.

Dragon droppings are often thought of as having almost magical powers. Droppings can glow in the dark (Glow-worms, Slugbulbs) They can give off an appalling smell (Stink Dragin, Rhinoback) They can drift through the air, as light as cobwebs, (Dreamserpent)

Hogfly

Puggle

Bullingdozer

Glow-worm

Giant Bee-Eater

Breathquencher

Wolf-fang

Prickleboggle

Water Dragon

Monstrous Nightmare

Bullrougher

Venomous Vorpent

Skullion

Rocket Ripper

Deadly Shadow

Gronckle

Stink Dragon

Rhinoback

Centidile

DRAGON POOS
(and How to Deal with Them)

Sometimes there is something about a dropping that tells you that you should RUN AWAY as fast as you possibly can...

THE MIGHTY MONSTERS

Of all the dragon species, the least is known about the Sea Dragons. How many Viking warriors have set sail with high hopes and brave hearts, only to be blasted straight to Valhalla by these mighty monsters, arising out of the sea like underwater mountains, blowing tornados from their nostrils, and hell-fire from their mouths? The water supports creatures of such extraordinary size, that they could never exist on land.

The largest of all is the Seadragonus Giganticus Maximus, a truly remarkable creature, that can whip up the ocean into waves twenty feet high with its gigantic tail, and shoot fire and electric lightning from its mouth and from its eyes. Little is known about the hundreds of other Sea Dragons, but in the pages that follow I have pieced together what I can from my own experiences and the stories of shipwrecked Vikings who lived to tell the tale…

Sea Dragons

Golphins

Golphins are friendly, intelligent creatures. Packs of Golphins often play around Viking boats and have been known to guide lost boats to safety. Golphins that have become separated from their pod sing a haunting song that seamen once thought was the song of ghosts.

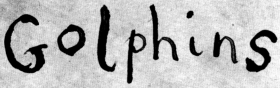

Make friends with a Golphin and they never forget

Swimming with Golphins is a great experience.

Fear Factor : 0
Attack : 2
Speed : 10
Size : 4
Disobedience : 6

Winterfleshers

Fear Factor : 6   Size : 2
Attack : 7   Disobedience : 7
Speed : 5

A Winterflesher is a tiny dragon about the length of your middle finger. With their mouths shut they look quite sweet, but actually they are a little like piranhas. When they attack in shoals they can strip a deer down to its skeleton in precisely three minutes.

Avoid them at all costs.

SNAP!

SNAP!.

SNAP!

The Monster of the Amber Slavelands

Fear Factor: 9
Attack: 9
Speed: 8
Size: 8
Disobedience: 9

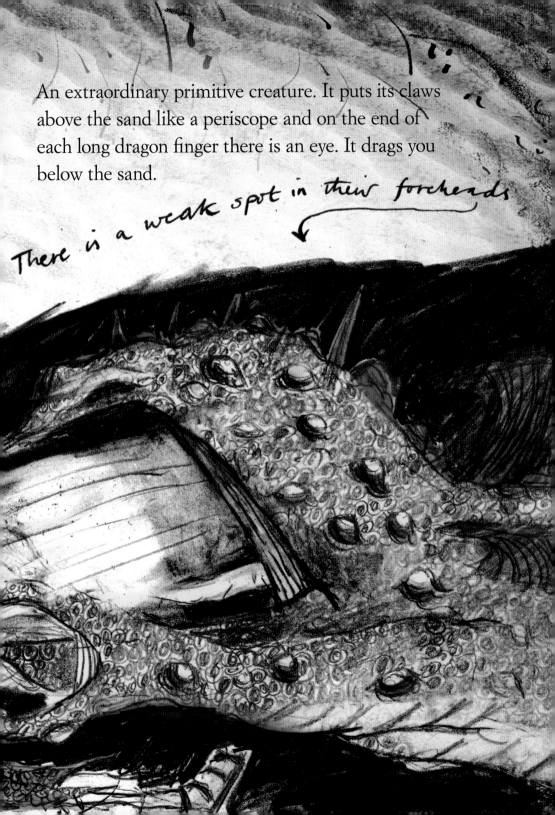

An extraordinary primitive creature. It puts its claws above the sand like a periscope and on the end of each long dragon finger there is an eye. It drags you below the sand.

There is a weak spot in their foreheads

Brainless Leg-Remover

Fear Factor: 5   **Size:** 1
Attack: 4   **Disobedience:** 7
Speed: 2

Brainless Leg-Removers are primitive creatures that
lurk beneath the sands of the Amber Slavelands.
Any sign of movement on the sands above
causes them to launch upwards and snap
shut their powerful clam-like jaws,
and then descend back down into
the depths of the
sand again.

Doomfangs

Fear Factor : 9
Attack : 9
Speed : 8

Size : 9
Disobedience : 9

Doomfangs are large, but strangely beautiful loners. If attacked, they will retaliate with a mysterious blue flame that freezes on contact. Doomfangs live way out in the Open Ocean and not much is known about them.

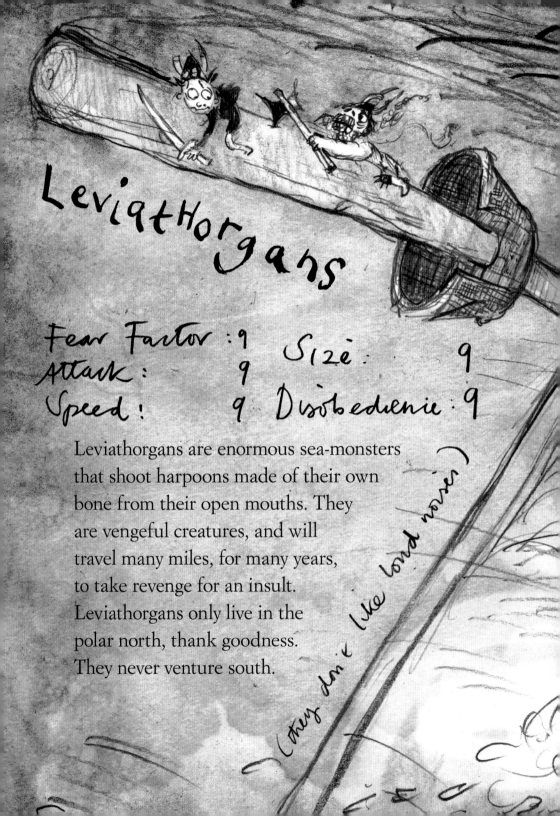

Leviathorgans

Fear Factor : 9   **Size :**   9
Attack :   9
Speed !   9   **Disobedience : 9**

Leviathorgans are enormous sea-monsters
that shoot harpoons made of their own
bone from their open mouths. They
are vengeful creatures, and will
travel many miles, for many years,
to take revenge for an insult.
Leviathorgans only live in the
polar north, thank goodness.
They never venture south.

(they don't like loud noises)

Darkbreathers

Fear Factor: 9   **Size: 9**
Attack: 9   **Disobedience: 9**
Speed: 6

Darkbreathers dwell at the very bottom of the ocean depths. They have lived so long in that icy ocean darkness, that their hearts have slowed to a terrible coldness, and they have a pathetic longing for the light. Darkbreathers can be attracted by the lanterns swinging from Viking ships, with gruesome results, as they have been known to swallow ships whole. They live on the ocean floor.

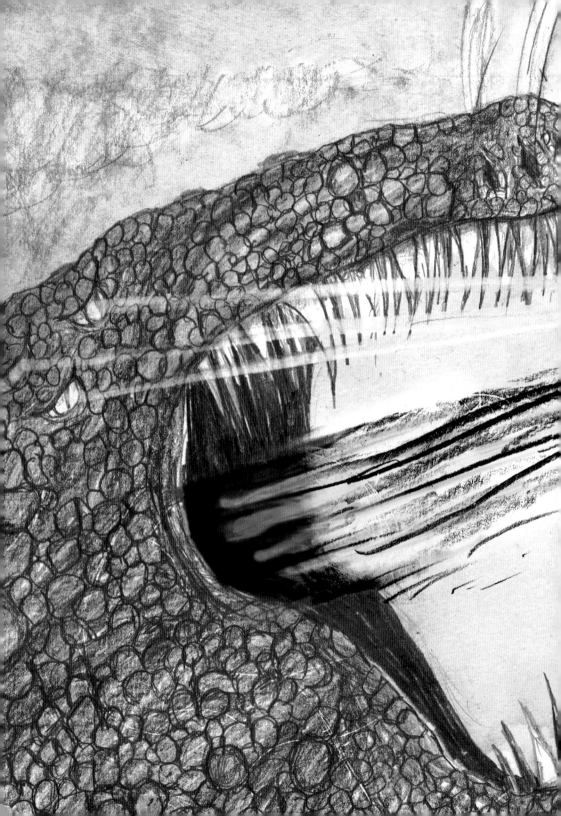

Woden's Nightmares

Fear Factor : 9
Attack : 9
Speed : 6

Size : 9
Disobedience : 9

Woden's Nightmares are unbelievably scary. I have no idea what to do about them.

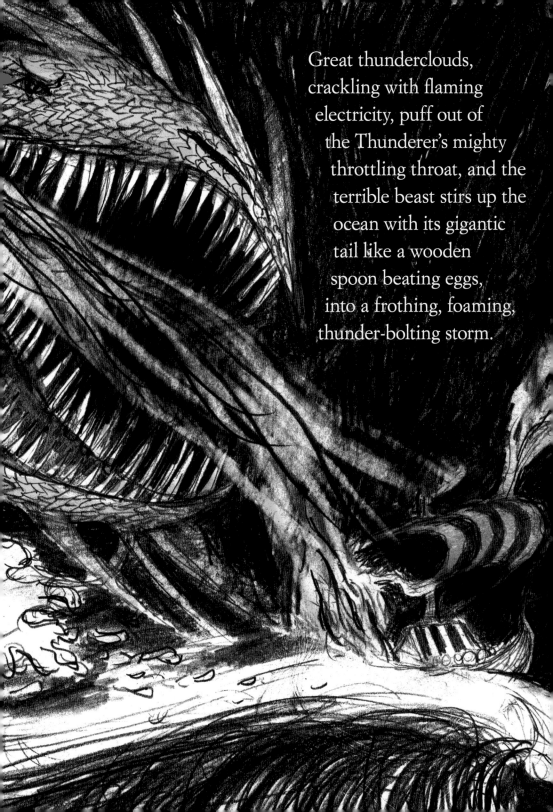

Great thunderclouds,
crackling with flaming
electricity, puff out of
the Thunderer's mighty
throttling throat, and the
terrible beast stirs up the
ocean with its gigantic
tail like a wooden
spoon beating eggs,
into a frothing, foaming,
thunder-bolting storm.

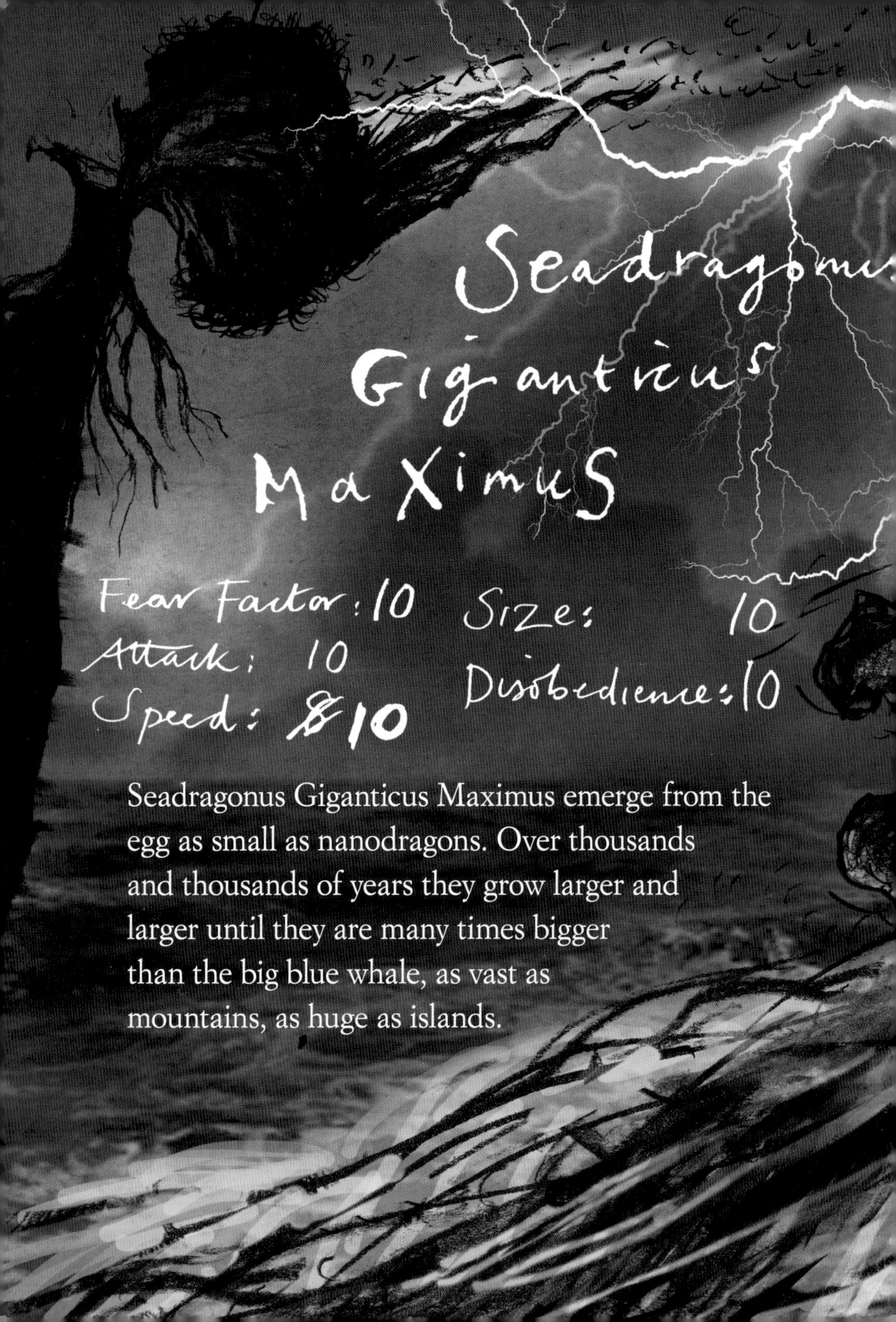

Seadragonus Giganticus Maximus

Fear Factor: 10

Attack: 10

Speed: ~~8~~ 10

Size: 10

Disobedience: 10

Seadragonus Giganticus Maximus emerge from the egg as small as nanodragons. Over thousands and thousands of years they grow larger and larger until they are many times bigger than the big blue whale, as vast as mountains, as huge as islands.

Furiosa is teaching me how to live in FIRE...

THE FUTURE of DRAGONS

I know now that we are standing on the edge of extinction, of either humans or dragons.

For a mighty Seadragonus Giganticus Maximus, the Dragon Furious, has risen up against the humans, and called upon his fellow dragon species to join together in a Dragon Rebellion whose aim is nothing less than the extinction of the entire human race. My arch-enemy, Alvin the Treacherous, has taken command of the human beings, and he is fighting back with all the fiendish and explosive weaponry that the dark inventive side of the human mind can devise.

Windwalker and Toothless have taught me how to live in water, earth and air. Now the Dragon Furious is teaching me how to live in FIRE...

I am writing these words from an underground tree hideout, and outside this place of safety, the Dragon Rebellion, and the humans under Alvin, will not rest until they have obliterated each other.

But I am still hopeful that I can step in somehow, prevent this calamity from happening, and begin a new world in which humans and dragons can live together peacefully.

I do not yet know the end of this story. The War has driven me, like a Windwalker, into an underground chrysalis, and outside this quiet place, a new world is evolving. I must break out of my hiding place, and strive to make this new world worthy of both our species. Not our species as they *are*, but as they *could be*.

I cannot imagine a future without dragons. I do not want a world in which our cave systems are dead, dark universes, inhabited only by bats and echoes. I do not want a world where I am wingless, crawling in the mud rather than reaching for the stars.

I do not want a world without Toothless.

I know it is only I who can save or destroy the dragons

now that Doomsday is approaching. But I do not know how to do it. How can I, when I am so small, so alone, and so great is the tangled web of hatred and destruction between our two species?

There must be a way... There must be a way...

Last night I dreamed of a fierce god of war and sea, tossing in his hands a mighty double-headed Axe of Doom across the skies ruined ragged by the War. Down below the mighty multitudes of men and of dragons craned their necks upward to see which way the axe will fall... *Which way will it fall for me?* thinks every individual. *Will it fall on the bright side or the dark?*

But more is at stake here than the fate of individuals. Will it be the humans or the dragons who survive?

O great and mighty Thor, let my thoughts have wings, bring fire and fangs to my imagination, so I can find out the answer, step in and catch the axe of Doom before it falls, and dream a little longer in this world full of dragons...

Know Your Dragons

The key below will tell you everything you need
to know about each dragon species.

 Human side in
the Rebellion

 Driving-
Dragon

 Dragon side
in the Rebellion

 Riding-
Dragon

 Super Eyesight

 Acid Blood

 Electric shocks
or lightning bolts

 Dangerous
gases

 Super Hearing

 Extra-scary
TEETH

 Speaks Norse

 X-ray vision

 Hunting-Dragon

 Non-Trainable
BEWARE!!

Can have more
than one head

 Poisonous

 telepathic

 VERY
LARGE

 Extra-scary
talons or horns

Neutral in
the Rebellion

 Lasers or missiles

 Hypnotic
powers

Speaks
Dragonese

 Speedy

 Chameleon

 sniff
sniff
 Super smell

 Can look
into the Future

CAVE DRAGONS

BRAIN PICKERS									
DRILLER-DRAGONS									
EIGHT-LEGGED NADDERS									
ELECTRICSTICKIES									
FLAMEHUFFERS									
GLOW-WORMS									
GRONCKLES									
RED-HOT ITCHYWORMS									
RIPROARERS									
SKULLIONS									
SLUGBULBS									
STICKYWORMS									
STRANGULATORS									

TREE DRAGONS

BREATHQUENCHERS									
BULLINGDOZERS									

CUCKOO DRAGONS									
DREAMSERPENTS									
FIRESTARTERS									
GIANT BEE-EATERS									
POISON DARTERS									
RED TIGERS									
SCARERS									
SHORTWING SQUIRRELSERPENTS									
VAMPIRE DRAGONS									
VAMPIRE SPYDRAGONS									
WOLF-FANGS									

BOG DRAGONS

ARSENIC ADDERWINGS									
BIG SPOTTED GORMLESS									
COMMON-OR-GARDEN DRAGONS									
EIGHT-LEGGED BATTLEGORES									
FLASHFANGS									

FLYING GATORS									
GLOOMERS									
HYPNOMUNKS									
LONG-EARED CARETAKER DRAGONS									
MARSH TIGERS									
MONSTROUS NIGHTMARES									
POISONOUS PIFFLEWORMS									
RHINOBACKS									
SIDEWINDERS									
SQUEALERS									
STINK DRAGONS									
TOXIC NIGHTSHADES									
VENOMOUS VORPENTS									

NANODRAGONS

CENTIDILES									
DROWSY-TIPPED DRAGONMICE									
ELECTRICSQUIRMS									

Dragon									
EMPEROR BEETLEBOOG BOLDERBUGS									
FLUTTERFIRES (inc. Long-Eared)									
PLANKENTEENIES									
PRICKLEBOGGLES									
TIDDLYNIP TICK BOTHERERS									

MOUNTAIN DRAGONS

Dragon									
BULLGUARD SLAVEDRAGONS									
DEADLY SHADOWS									
EXTERMINATORS									
GRIMLERS									
HOGFLYS									
MOOD-DRAGONS									
PUGGLES									
RAPTORTONGUES									
RAZORWINGS									
SNIFFER DRAGONS									
SNUBBED-NOSED HELLSTEETHERS									

SPECKLEHOUNDS									
STEALTH DRAGONS									
TONGUE-TWISTERS									

SKY DRAGONS

BULLROUGHERS									
CHICKEN POXERS									
DEVILISH DERVISH									
RAVENHUNTERS									
ROCKET RIPPERS									
SILVER PHANTOMS									
TRIPLE-HEADER RAGEBLASTS									
TWO-HEADED GORMATRONS									
WINDWALKERS									
ZEBRAMOUNTS									

SEA DRAGONS

BRAINLESS LEG-REMOVERS									
DARKBREATHERS									

DOOMFANGS										
DREADERS										
GOLPHINS										
HORRORS										
LEVIATHORGANS										
POLAR-SERPENTS										
SABRE-TOOTH DRIVER DRAGONS										
SAVAGERS										
SEADRAGONUS GIGANTICUS MAXIMUS										
SHARKWORMS										
THE MONSTER OF THE AMBER SLAVELANDS										
THOR'S THUNDERERS										
WINTERFLESHERS										
WODEN'S NIGHTMARE										

~ WHERE TO FIND THE DRAGONS ~

You can read lots more about the dragons in Hiccup's memoirs. Here's where you'll find some of them:

How to Train Your Dragon

Seadragonus Giganticus Maximus,
Common-or-Garden or Basic Brown Dragon,
Monstrous Nightmare, Gronckle

How to Be a Pirate

Monstrous Strangulator, Skullions,
Deadly Nadders, Electricsquirms

How to Speak Dragonese

Sharkworms, Electricsquirms, Emperor Beetleboog Bolderbug,
Monstrous Nightmare, Gronckle, Venomous Vorpents

How to Cheat a Dragon's Curse

Venomous Vorpent, Squealers,
Sabre-tooth Driver Dragons, Doomfang

How to Twist a Dragon's Tale

Exterminators, Water Dragons, Chickenpoxer,
Windwalkers, Rocket Rippers

A Hero's Guide to Deadly Dragons
Poisonous Piffleworms, Stealth dragons, Driller-Dragons,
Squirrelserpents, Mood-dragon, Red-Hot Itchyworms

How to Ride a Dragon's Storm
Polar-serpents, Leviathorgan, Mood-dragon, Raptortongues

How to Break a Dragon's Heart
Poison Darters, Scarers, Giant Bee-Eaters,
Seadragonus Giganticus Maximus

How to Steal a Dragon's Sword
Tongue-twisters, Seadragonus Giganticus Maximus,
Flamehuffers, Riproarers, Stickyworms

How to Seize a Dragon's Jewel
The Monster of the Amber Slavelands, Brainless Leg-Remover,
Triple-Header Deadly Shadow, Silver Phantoms,
Seadragonus Giganticus Maximus,
Long-Eared Caretaker Dragons

How to Betray a Dragon's Hero
Vampire Spydragons, Winterfleshers, Hogflys,
Bullguard Slavedragons, Seadragonus Giganticus Maximus

Cressida, age 9, writing on the little island that
was the inspiration for the isle of Berk.

The past is another country.
They do things differently there...